The Devotee And Other Short Stories, By Rabindranatn Tagore

The short story is often viewed as an inferior relation to the Novel. But it is an art in itself. To take a story and distil its essence into fewer pages while keeping character and plot rounded and driven is not an easy task. Many try and many fail.

In this series we look at short stories from many of our most accomplished writers. Miniature masterpieces with a lot to say. In this volume we examine some of the short stories of Rabindranath Tagore.

And with him we venture to the East. To meet the poet and story teller who speaks a common language of love and mysticism which continues to convey valuable insights into universal themes in contemporary society.

Rabindranath Tagore (1861-1941) who was a gifted Bengali Renaissance man, distinguishing himself as a philosopher, social and political reformer and a popular author in all literary genres. He was instrumental in an increased freedom for the press and influenced Gandhi and the founders of modern India.

He composed hundreds of songs which are still sung today as they include the Indian and Bangladesh's national anthems.

His prolific literary life has left a legacy of quality novels, essays and in this volume his shorter works.

Gitanjali, one of his most famous works, earned him the distinction of being the first Asian writer to receive the Nobel Prize in Literature in 1913.

At the end of the poems you will find a longer biography of Tagore, specially written for this volume.

Many of the poems are also available as an audiobook from our sister company Portable Poetry. Many samples are at our youtube channel http://www.youtube.com/user/PortablePoetry?feature=mhee The full volume can be purchased from iTunes, Amazon and other digital stores. Among our readers are Shyama Perera and Ghizela Rowe

Index Of Stories

The Devotee

At a time, when my unpopularity with a part of my readers had reached the nadir of its glory, and my name had become the central orb of the journals, to be attended through space with a perpetual rotation of revilement, I felt the necessity to retire to some quiet place and endeavour to forget my own existence.

I have a house in the country some miles away from Calcutta, where I can remain unknown and unmolested. The villagers there have not, as yet, come to any conclusion about me. They know I am no mere holiday-maker or pleasure-seeker; for I never outrage the silence of the village nights with the riotous noises of the city. Nor do they regard me as ascetic, because the little acquaintance they have of me carries the savour of comfort about it. I am not, to them, a traveller; for, though I am a vagabond by nature, my wandering through the village fields is aimless. They are hardly even quite certain whether I am married or single; for they have never seen me with my children. So, not being able to classify me in any animal or vegetable kingdom that they know, they have long since given me up and left me stolidly alone.

But quite lately I have come to know that there is one person in the village who is deeply interested in me. Our acquaintance began on a sultry afternoon in July. There had been rain all the morning, and the air was still wet and heavy with mist, like eyelids when weeping is over.

I sat lazily watching a dappled cow grazing on the high bank of the river. The afternoon sun was playing on her glossy hide. The simple beauty of this dress of light made me wonder idly at man's deliberate waste of money in setting up tailors' shops to deprive his own skin of its natural clothing.

While I was thus watching and lazily musing, a woman of middle age came and prostrated herself before me, touching the ground with her forehead. She carried in her robe some bunches of flowers, one of which she offered to me with folded hands. She said to me, as she offered it: "This is an offering to my God."

She went away. I was so taken aback as she uttered these words, that I could hardly catch a glimpse of her before she was gone. The whole incident was entirely simple, but it left a deep impression on my mind; and as I turned back once more to look at the cattle in the field, the zest of life in the cow, who was munching the lush grass with deep breaths, while she whisked off the flies, appeared to me fraught with mystery. My readers may laugh at my foolishness, but my heart was full of adoration. I offered my worship to the pure joy of living, which is God's own life. Then, plucking a tender shoot from the mango tree, I fed the cow with it from my own hand, and as I did this I had the satisfaction of having pleased my God.

The next year when I returned to the village it was February. The cold season still lingered on. The morning sun came into my room, and I was grateful for its warmth. I was writing, when the servant came to tell me that a devotee, of the Vishnu cult, wanted to see me. I told him, in an absent way, to bring her upstairs, and went on with my writing. The Devotee came in, and bowed to me, touching my feet. I found that she was the same woman whom I had met, for a brief moment, a year ago.

I was able now to examine her more closely. She was past that age when one asks the question whether a woman is beautiful or not. Her stature was above the ordinary height, and she was strongly built; but her body was slightly bent owing to her constant attitude of veneration. Her manner had nothing shrinking about it. The most remarkable of her features were her two eyes. They seemed to have a penetrating power which could make distance near.

With those two large eyes of hers, she seemed to push me as she entered.

"What is this?" she asked. "Why have you brought me here before your throne, my God? I used to see you among the trees; and that was much better. That was the true place to meet you."

She must have seen me walking in the garden without my seeing her. For the last few clays, however, I had suffered from a cold, and had been prevented from going out. I had, perforce, to stay indoors and pay my homage to the evening sky from my terrace. After a silent pause the Devotee said to me: "O my God, give me some words of good."

I was quite unprepared for this abrupt request, and answered her on the spur of the moment: "Good words I neither give nor receive. I simply open my eyes and keep silence, and then I can at once both hear and see, even when no sound is uttered. Now, while I am looking at you, it is as good as listening to your voice."

The Devotee became quite excited as I spoke, and exclaimed: "God speaks to me, not only with His mouth, but with His whole body."

I said to her: "When I am silent I can listen with my whole body. I have come away from Calcutta here to listen to that sound."

The Devotee said: "Yes, I know that, and therefore 1 have come here to sit by you."

Before taking her leave, she again bowed to me, and touched my feet. I could see that she was distressed, because my feet were covered. She wished them to be bare.

Early next morning I came out, and sat on my terrace on the roof. Beyond the line of trees southward I could see the open country chill and desolate. I could watch the sun rising over the sugar-cane in the East, beyond the clump of trees at the side of the village. Out of the deep shadow of those dark trees the village road suddenly appeared. It stretched forward, winding its way to some distant villages on the horizon, till it was lost in the grey of the mist.

That morning it was difficult to say whether the sun had risen or not. A white fog was still clinging to the tops of the trees. I saw the Devotee walking through the blurred dawn, like a mist-wraith of the morning twilight. She was singing her chant to God, and sounding her cymbals.

The thick haze lifted at last; and the sun, like the kindly grandsire of the village, took his seat amid all the work that was going on in home and field.

When I had just settled down at my writing-table, to appease the hungry appetite of my editor in Calcutta, there came a sound of footsteps on the stair, and the Devotee, humming a tune to herself, entered, and bowed before me. I lifted my head from my papers.

She said to me: "My God, yesterday I took as sacred food what was left over from your meal."

I was startled, and asked her how she could do that.

"Oh," she said, "I waited at your door in the evening, while you were at dinner, and took some food from your plate when it was carried out."

This was a surprise to me, for everyone in the village knew that I had been to Europe, and had eaten with Europeans. I was a vegetarian, no doubt, but the sanctity of my cook would not bear investigation, and the orthodox regarded my food as polluted.

The Devotee, noticing my sign of surprise, said: "My God, why should I come to you at all, if I could not take your food?"

I asked her what her own caste people would say. She told me she had already spread the news far and wide all over the village. The caste people had shaken their heads, but agreed that she must go her own way.

I found out that the Devotee came from a good family in the country, and that her mother was well to-do, and desired to keep her daughter. But she preferred to be a mendicant. I asked her how she made her living. She told me that her followers had given her a piece of land, and that she begged her food from door to door. She said to me: "The food which I get by begging is divine."

After I had thought over what she said, I understood her meaning. When we get our food precariously as alms, we remember God the giver. But when we receive our food regularly at home, as a matter of course, we are apt to regard it as ours by right.

I had a great desire to ask her about her husband. But as she never mentioned him even indirectly, I did not question her.

I found out very soon that the Devotee had no respect at all for that part of the village where the people of the higher castes lived.

"They never give," she said, "a single farthing to God's service; and yet they have the largest share of God's glebe. But the poor worship and starve."

I asked her why she did not go and live among these godless people, and help them towards a better life. "That," I said with some unction, "would be the highest form of divine worship."

I had heard sermons of this kind from time to time, and I am rather fond of copying them myself for the public benefit, when the chance comes.

But the Devotee was not at all impressed. She raised her big round eyes, and looked straight into mine, and said:

"You mean to say that because God is with the sinners, therefore when you do them any service you do it to God? Is that so?"

"Yes," I replied, "that is my meaning."

"Of course," she answered almost impatiently, "of course, God is with them: otherwise, how could they go on living at all? But what is that to me? My God is not there. My God cannot be worshipped among them; because I do not find Him there. I seek Him where I can find Him."

As she spoke, she made obeisance to me. What she meant to say was really this. A mere doctrine of God's omnipresence does not help us. That God is all-pervading, this truth may be a mere intangible abstraction, and therefore unreal to ourselves. Where I can see Him, there is His reality in my soul.

I need not explain that all the while she showered her devotion on me she did it to me not as an individual. I was simply a vehicle of her divine worship. It was not for me either to receive it or to refuse it: for it was not mine, but God's.

When the Devotee came again, she found me once more engaged with my books and papers.

"What have you been doing," she said, with evident vexation, "that my God should make you undertake such drudgery? Whenever I come, I find you reading and writing."

"God keeps his useless people busy," I answered; "otherwise they would be bound to get into mischief. They have to do all the least necessary things in life. It keeps them out of trouble."

The Devotee told me that she could not bear the encumbrances, with which, day by day, I was surrounded. If she wanted to see me, she was not allowed by the servants to come straight upstairs. If she wanted to touch my feet in worship, there were my socks always in the way. And when she wanted to have a simple talk with me, she found my mind lost in a wilderness of letters.

This time, before she left me, she folded her hands, and said: "My God! I felt your feet in my breast this morning. Oh, how cool! And they were bare, not covered. I held them upon my head for a long time in worship. That filled my very being. Then, after that, pray what was the use of my coming to you yourself? Why did I come? My Lord, tell me truly, wasn't it a mere infatuation?"

There were some flowers in my vase on the table. While she was there, the gardener brought some new flowers to put in their place. The Devotee saw him changing them.

"Is that all?" she exclaimed. "Have you done with the flowers? Then give them to me."

She held the flowers tenderly in the cup of her hands, and began to gaze at them with bent head. After a few moments' silence she raised her head again, and said to me: "You never look at these flowers; therefore they become stale to you. If you would only look into them, then your reading and writing would go to the winds."

She tied the flowers together in the end of her robe, and placed them, in an attitude of worship, on the top of her head, saying reverently: "Let me carry my God with me."

While she did this, I felt that flowers in our rooms do not receive their due meed of loving care at our hands. When we stick them in vases, they are more like a row of naughty schoolboys standing on a form to be punished.

The Devotee came again the same evening, and sat by my feet on the terrace of the roof.

"I gave away those flowers," she said, "as I went from house to house this morning, singing God's name. Beni, the head man of our village, laughed at me for my devotion, and said: `Why do you waste all this devotion on Him? Don't you know He is reviled up and down the countryside?' Is that true, my God? Is it true that they are hard upon you?"

For a moment I shrank into myself. It was a shock to find that the stains of printers' ink could reach so far.

The Devotee went on: "Beni imagined that he could blow out the flame of my devotion at one breath! But this is no mere tiny flame: it is a burning fire. Why do they abuse you, my God?"

I said: "Because I deserved it. I suppose in my greed I was loitering about to steal people's hearts in secret."

The Devotee said: "Now you see for yourself how little their hearts are worth. They are full of poison, and this will cure you of your greed."

"When a man," I answered, "has greed in his heart, he is always on the verge of being beaten. The greed itself supplies his enemies with poison."

"Our merciful God," she replied, "beats us with His own hand, and drives away all the poison. He who endures God's beating to the end is saved."

II.

That evening the Devotee told me the story of her life. The stars of evening rose and set behind the trees, as she went on to the end of her tale.

"My husband is very simple. Some people think that he is a simpleton; but I know that those who understand simply, understand truly. In business and household management he was able to hold his own. Because his needs were small, and his wants few, he could manage carefully on what we had. He would never meddle in other matters, nor try to understand them.

"Both my husband's parents died before we had been married long, and we were left alone. But my husband always needed some one to be over him. I am ashamed to confess that he had a sort of reverence for me, and looked upon me as his superior. But I am sure that he could understand things better than I, though I had greater powers of talking.

"Of all the people in the world he held his Guru Thakur (spiritual master) in the highest veneration. Indeed it was not veneration merely but love; and such love as his is rare.

"Guru Thakur was younger than my husband. Oh! how beautiful he was!

"My husband had played games with him when he was a boy; and from that time forward he had dedicated his heart and soul to this friend of his early days. Thakur knew how simple my husband was, and used to tease him mercilessly.

"He and his comrades would play jokes upon him for their own amusement; but he would bear them all with longsuffering.

"When I married into this family, Guru Thakur was studying at Benares. My husband used to pay all his expenses. I was eighteen years old when he returned home to our village.

"At the age of fifteen I had my child. I was so young I did not know how to take care of him. I was fond of gossip, and liked to be with my village friends for hours together. I used to get quite cross with my boy when I was compelled to stay at home and nurse him. Alas! my child-God came into my life, but His playthings were not ready for Him. He came to the mother's heart, but the mother's heart lagged behind. He left me in anger; and ever since I have been searching for Him up and down the world.

"The boy was the joy of his father's life. My careless neglect used to pain my husband. But his was a mute soul. He has never been able to give expression to his pain.

"The wonderful thing was this, that in spite of my neglect the child used to love me more than anyone else. He seemed to have the dread that I would one day go away and leave him. So even when I was with him, he would watch me with a restless look in his eyes. He had me very little to himself, and therefore his desire to be with me was always painfully eager. When I went each day to the river, he used to fret and stretch out his little arms to be taken with me. But the bathing ghal was my place for meeting my friends, and I did not care to burden myself with the child.

"It was an early morning in August. Fold after fold of grey clouds had wrapped the mid-day round with a wet clinging robe. I asked the maid to take care of the boy, while I went down to the river. The child cried after me as I went away.

"There was no one there at the bathing ghat when I arrived. As a swimmer, I was the best among all the village women. The river was quite full with the rains. I swam out into the middle of the stream some distance from the shore.

"Then I heard a cry from the bank, 'Mother!' I turned my head and saw my boy coming down the steps, calling me as he came. I shouted to him to stop, but he went on, laughing and calling. My feet and hands became cramped with fear. I shut my eyes, afraid to see. When I opened them, there, at the slippery stairs, my boy's ripple of laughter had disappeared for ever.

"I got back to the shore. I raised him from the water. I took him in my arms, my boy, my darling, who had begged so often in vain for me to take him. I took him now, but he no more looked in my eyes and called ` Mother.'

"My child-God had come. I had ever neglected Him. I had ever made Him cry. And now all that neglect began to beat against my own heart, blow upon blow, blow upon blow. When my boy was with me, I had left him alone. I had refused to take him with me. And now, when he is dead, his memory clings to me and never leaves me.

"God alone knows all that my husband suffered. If he had only punished me for my sin, it would have been better for us both. But be knew only how to endure in silence, not how to speak.

"When I was almost mad with grief, Guru Thakur came back. In earlier days, the relation between him and my husband had been that of boyish friendship. Now, my husband's reverence for his sanctity and learning was unbounded. He could hardly speak in his presence, his awe of him was so great.

"My husband asked his Guru to try to give me some consolation. Guru Thakur began to read and explain to me the scriptures. But I do not think they had much effect on my mind. All their value for me lay in the voice that uttered them. God makes the draught of divine life deepest in the heart for man to drink, through the human voice. He has no better vessel in His hand than that; and He Himself drinks His divine draught out of the same vessel.

"My husband's love and veneration for his Guru filled our house, as incense fills a temple shrine. I showed that veneration, and had peace. I saw my God in the form of that Guru. He used to come to take his meal at our house every morning. The first thought that would come to my mind on waking from sleep was that of his food as a sacred gift from God. When I prepared the things for his meal, my fingers would sing for joy.

"When my husband saw my devotion to his Guru, his respect for me greatly increased. He noticed his Guru's eager desire to explain the scriptures to me. He used to think that he could never expect to earn any regard from his Guru himself, on account of his stupidity; but his wife had made up for it.

"Thus another five years went by happily, and my whole life would have passed like that; but beneath the surface some stealing was going on somewhere in secret. I could not detect it; but it was detected by the God of my heart. Then came a day when, in a moment our whole life was turned upside down.

"It was a morning in midsummer. I was returning home from bathing, my clothes all wet, down a shady lane. At the bend of the road, under the mango tree, I met my Guru Thakur. He had his towel on his shoulder and was repeating some Sanskrit verses as he was going to take his bath. With my wet clothes clinging all about me I was ashamed to meet him. I tried to pass by quickly, and avoid being seen. He called me by my name.

"I stopped, lowering my eyes, shrinking into myself. He fixed his gaze upon me, and said: `How beautiful is your body!'

"All the universe of birds seemed to break into song in the branches overhead. All the bushes in the lane seemed ablaze with flowers. It was as though the earth and sky and everything had become a riot of intoxicating joy.

"I cannot tell how I got home. I only remember that I rushed into the room where we worship God. But the room seemed empty. Only before my eyes those same gold spangles of light were dancing which had quivered in front of me in that shady lane on my way back from the river.

"Guru Thakur came to take his food that day, and asked my husband where I had gone. He searched for me, but could not find me anywhere.

"Ah! I have not the same earth now any longer. The same sunlight is not mine. I called on my God in my dismay, and He kept His face turned away from me.

"The day passed, I know not how. That night I had to meet my husband. But the night is dark and silent. It is the time when my husband's mind comes out shining, like stars at twilight. I had heard him speak things in the dark, and I had been surprised to find how deeply he understood.

"Sometimes I am late in the evening in going to rest on account of household work. My husband waits for me, seated on the floor, without going to bed. Our talk at such times had often begun with something about our Guru.

That night, when it was past midnight, I came to my room, and found my husband sleeping on the floor. Without disturbing him I lay down on the ground at his feet, my head towards him. Once he stretched his feet, while sleeping, and struck me on the breast. That was his last bequest.

"Next morning, when my husband woke up from his sleep, I was already sitting by him. Outside the window, over the thick foliage of the jack- fruit tree, appeared the first pale red of the dawn at the fringe of the night. It was so early that the crows had not yet begun to call.

"I bowed, and touched my husband's feet with my forehead. He sat up, starting as if waking from a dream, and looked at my face in amazement. I said:

"' I have made up my mind. I must leave the world. I cannot belong to you any longer. I must leave your home.'

"Perhaps my husband thought that he was still dreaming. He said not a word.

Ah! do hear me l' I pleaded with infinite pain. `Do hear me and understand I You must marry another wife. I must take my leave.'

"My husband said: ' What is all this wild, mad talk? Who advises you to leave the world?'

"I said: ` My Guru Thakur.'

"My husband looked bewildered. ' Guru Thakur!' he cried. ' When did he give you this advice?'

"`In the morning,' I answered, ' yesterday, when I met him on my way back from the river.'

"His voice trembled a little. He turned, and looked in my face, and asked me: `Why did he give you such a behest?'

"`I do not know,' I answered. ' Ask him 1 He will tell you himself, if he can.'

"My husband said: `It is possible to leave the world, even when continuing to live in it. You need not leave my home. I will speak to my Guru about it.'

"` Your Guru,' I said, ` may accept your petition; but my heart will never give its consent. I must leave your home. From henceforth, the world is no more to me.'

"My husband remained silent, and we sat there on the floor in the dark. When it was light, he said to me: ' Let us both came to him.'

"I folded my hands and said: ` I shall never meet him again.'

"He looked into my face. I lowered my eyes. He said no more. I knew that, somehow, he had seen into my mind, and understood what was there. In this world of mine, there were only two who loved me best-my boy and my husband. That love was my God, and therefore it could brook no falsehood. One of these two left me, and I left the other. Now I must have truth, and truth alone."

She touched the ground at my feet, rose and bowed to me, and departed.

"We Crown Thee King"

When Nabendu Sekhar was wedded to Arunlekha, the God of marriage smiled from behind the sacrificial fire. Alas! what is sport for the gods is not always a joke to us poor mortals.

Purnendu Sekhar, the father of Nabendu, was a man well known amongst the English officials of the Government. In the voyage of life he had arrived at the desert shores of Rai Bahadurship by diligently plying his oats of salaams. He held in reserve enough for further advancement, but at the age of fifty-five, his tender gaze still fixed on the misty peals of Raja-hood, he suddenly found himself transported to a region where earthly honours and decorations are naught, and his salaam-wearied neck found everlasting repose on the funeral pyre.

According to modern science, force is not destroyed, but is merely converted to another form, and applied to another point. So Purnendu's salaam-force, constant handmaid of the fickle Goddess of Fortune, descended from the shoulder of the father to that of his worthy son; and the youthful head of Nabendu Sekhar began to move up and down, at the doors of high-placed Englishmen, like a pumpkin swayed by the wind.

The traditions of the family into which he had married were entirely different. Its eldest son, Pramathanath, had won for himself the love of his kinsfolk and the regard of all who knew him. His kinsmen and his neighbours looked up to him as their ideal in all things.

Pramathanath was a Bachelor of Arts, and in addition was gifted with common sense. But he held no high official position; he had no handsome salary; nor did he exert any influence with his pen. There was no one in power to lend him a helping hand, because he desired to keep away from Englishmen, as much as they desired to keep away from him. So it happened that he shone only within the sphere of his family and his friends, and excited no admiration beyond it.

Yet this Pramathanath had once sojourned in England for some three years. The kindly treatment he received during his stay there overpowered him so much that he forgot the sorrow and the humiliation of his own country, and came back dressed in European clothes. This rather grieved his brothers and his sisters at first, but after a few days they began to think that European clothes suited nobody better, and gradually they came to share his pride and dignity.

On his return from England, Pramathanath resolved that he would show the world how to associate with Anglo-Indians on terms of equality. Those of our countrymen who think that no such association is possible, unless we bend our knees to them, showed their utter lack of self-respect, and were also unjust to the English-so thought Pramathanath.

He brought with him letters of introduction from many distinguished Englishmen at home, and these gave him some recognition in Anglo-Indian society. He and his wife occasionally enjoyed English hospitality at tea, dinner, sports and other entertainments. Such good luck intoxicated him, and began to produce a tingling sensation in every vein of his body.

About this time, at the opening of a new railway line, many of the town, proud recipients of official favour, were invited by the Lieutenant-Governor to take the first trip. Pramathanath was among them. On the return journey, a European Sergeant of the Police expelled some Indian gentlemen from a railway-carriage with great insolence. Pramathanath, dressed in his European clothes, was there.

He, too, was getting out, when the Sergeant said: "You needn't move, sir. Keep your seat, please."

At first Pramathanath felt flattered at the special respect thus shown to him. When, however, the train went on, the dull rays of the setting sun, at the west of the fields, now ploughed up and stripped of green, seemed in his eyes to spread a glow of shame over the whole country. Sitting near the window of his lonely compartment, he seemed to catch a glimpse of the down-cast eyes of his Motherland, hidden behind the trees. As Pramathanath sat there, lost in reverie, burning tears flowed down his cheeks, and his heart burst with indignation.

He now remembered the story of a donkey who was drawing the chariot of an idol along the street. The wayfarers bowed down to the idol, and touched the dusty ground with their foreheads. The foolish donkey imagined that all this reverence was being shown to him. "The only difference," said Pramathanath to himself, " between the donkey and myself is this: I understand to-day that the respect I receive is not given to me but to the burden on my back."

Arriving home, Pramathanath called together all the children of the household, and lighting a big bonfire, threw all his European clothes into it one by one. The children danced round and round it, and the higher the flames shot up, the greater was their merriment. After that, Pramathanath gave up his sip of tea and bits of toast in Anglo-Indian houses, and once again sat inaccessible within the castle of his house, while his insulted friends went about from the door of one Englishman to that of another, bending their turbaned heads as before.

By an irony of fate, poor Nabendu Sekhar married the second daughter of this house. His sisters-in-law were well educated and handsome. Nabendu considered he had made a lucky bargain. But he lost no time in trying to impress on the family that it was a rare bargain on their side also. As if by mistake, he would often hand to his sisters-in-law sundry letters that his late father had received from Europeans. And when the cherry lips of those young ladies smiled sarcastically, and the point of a shining dagger peeped out of its sheath of red velvet, the unfortunate man saw his folly, and regretted it.

Labanyalekha, the eldest sister, surpassed the rest in beauty and cleverness. Finding an auspicious day, she put on the mantel-shelf of Nabendu's bedroom two pairs of English boots, daubed with vermilion, and arranged flowers, sandal-paste, incense and a couple of burning candles before them in true ceremonial fashion. When Nabendu came in, the two sisters-in-law stood on either side of him, and said with mock solemnity: "Bow down to your gods, and may you prosper through their blessings."

The third sister Kiranlekha spent many days in embroidering with red silk one hundred common English names such as Jones, Smith, Brown, Thomson, etc., on a chadar. When it was ready, she presented this namavoli (A namavoli is a sheet of cloth printed all over with the names of Hindu gods and goddesses and worn by pious Hindus when engaged in devotional exercises.) to Nabendu Sekhar with great ceremony.

The fourth, Sasankalekha, of tender age and therefore of no account, said: "I will make you a string of beads, brother, with which to tell the names of your gods-the sahibs." Her sisters reproved her, saying: "Run away, you saucy girl."

Feelings of shame and irritation assailed by turns the mind of Nabendu Sekhar. Still he could not forego the company of his sisters-in-law, especially as the eldest one was beautiful. Her honey was no less than her gall, and Nabendu's mind tasted at once the sweetness of the one and the bitterness of the other. The butterfly, with its bruised wings, buzzes round the flower in blind fury, unable to depart.

The society of his sisters-in-Law so much infatuated him that at last Nabendu began to disavow his craving for European favours. When he went to salaam the Burra Sahib, he used to pretend that he was going to listen to a speech by Mr. Surendranath Banerjea. When he went to the railway station to pay respects to the Chota Sahib, returning from Darjeeling, he would tell his sisters-in-law that he expected his youngest uncle.

It was a sore trial to the unhappy man placed between the cross-fires of his Sahibs and his sisters-in-law. The sisters-in-law, however, secretly vowed that they would not rest till the Sahibs had been put to rout.

About this time it was rumoured that Nabendu's name would be included in the forthcoming list of Birthday honours, and that he would mount the first step of the ladder to Paradise by becoming a Rai Bahadur. The poor fellow had not the courage to break the joyful news to his sisters-in-law. One evening, however, when the autumn moon was flooding the earth with its mischievous beams, Nabendu's heart was so full that he could not contain himself any longer, and he told his wife. The next day, Mrs. Nabendu betook herself to her eldest sister's house in a palanquin, and in a voice choked with tears bewailed her lot.

"He isn't going to grow a tail," said Labanya, "by becoming a Rai Bahadur, is he? Why should you feel so very humiliated? "

"Oh, no, sister dear," replied Arunlekha, "I am prepared to be anything but not a Rai-Baha-durni." The fact was that in her circle of acquaintances there was one Bhutnath Babu, who was a Rai Bahadur, and that explained her intense aversion to that title.

Labanya said to her sister in soothing tones: "Don't be upset about it, dear; I will see what I can do to prevent it"

Babu Nilratan, the husband of Labanya, was a pleader at Buxar. When the autumn was over, Nabendu received an invitation from Labanya to pay them a visit, and he started for Buxar greatly pleased.

The early winter of the western province endowed Labanyalekha with new health and beauty, and brought a glowing colour to her pale cheeks, She looked like the flower-laden kasa reeds on a clear autumn day, growing by the lonely bank of a rivulet. To Nabendu's enchanted eyes she appeared like a malati plant in full blossom, showering dew-drops brilliant with the morning light.

Nabendu had never felt better in his life. The exhilaration of his own health and the genial company of his pretty sister-in-law made him think himself light enough to tread on air. The Ganges in front of the garden seemed to him to be flowing ceaselessly to regions unknown, as though it gave shape to his own wild fantasies.

As he returned in the early morning from his walk on the bank of the river, the mellow rays of the winter sun gave his whole frame that pleasing sensation of warmth which lovers feel in each other's arms. Coming home, he would now and then find his sister-in-Law amusing herself by cooking some dishes. He would offer his help, and display his want of skill and ignorance at every step. But Nabendu did not appear to be at all anxious to improve himself by practice and attention. On the contrary he thoroughly enjoyed the rebukes he received from his sister-in-law. He was at great pains to prove every day that he was inefficient and helpless as a new-born babe in mixing spices, handling the saucepan, and regulating the heat so as to prevent things getting burnt-and he was duly rewarded with pitiful smiles and scoldings.

In the middle of the day he ate a great deal of the good food set before him, incited by his keen appetite and the coaxing of his sister-in-law. Later on, he would sit down to a game of cards, at which he betrayed the same lack of ability. He would cheat, pry into his adversary's hand, quarrel but never did he win a single rubber, and worse still, he would not acknowledge defeat. This brought him abuse every day, and still he remained incorrigible.

There was, however, one matter in which his reform was complete. For the time at least, he had forgotten that to win the smiles of Sahibs was the final goal of life. He was beginning to understand how happy and worthy we might feel by winning the affection and esteem of those near and dear to us.

Besides, Nabendu was now moving in a new atmosphere. Labanya's husband, Babu Nilratan, a leader of the bar, was reproached by many, because he refused to pay his respects to European officials. To all such reproaches Nilratan would reply: "No, thank you, if they are not polite enough to return my call, then the politeness I offer them is a loss that can never be made up for. The sands of the desert may be very white and shiny, but I would much rather sow my seeds in black soil, where I can expect a return."

And Nabendu began to adopt similar ideas, all regardless of the future. His chance of Rai Bahadurship throve on the soil carefully prepared by his late father and also by himself in days gone by, nor was any fresh watering required. Had he not at great expense laid out a splendid race-course in a town, which was a fashionable resort of Europeans?

When the time of Congress drew near, Nilratan received a request from head-quarters to collect subscriptions. Nabendu, free from anxiety, was merrily engaged in a game of cards with his sister-in. law, when Nilratan Babu came upon him with a subscription-book in his hand, and said: "Your signature, please."

From old habit Nabendu looked horrified. Labanya, assuming an air of great concern and anxiety, said: "Never do that. It would ruin your racecourse beyond repair."

Nabendu blurted out: "Do you suppose I pass sleepless nights through fear of that?"

"We won't publish your name in the papers," said Nilratan reassuringly.

Labanya, looking grave and anxious, said: "Still, it wouldn't be safe. Things spread so, from mouth to mouth —"

Nabendu replied with vehemence: "My name wouldn't suffer by appearing in the newspapers." So saying, he snatched the subscription list from Nilratan's hand, and signed away a thousand rupees. Secretly he hoped that the papers would not publish the news.

Labanya struck her forehead with her palm and gasped out: What, have you, done?"

"Nothing wrong," said Nabendu boastfully.

"But—but," drawled Labanya, "the Guard sahib of Sealdah Station, the shop-assistant at Whiteaway's, the syce-sahib of Hart Bros. these gentlemen might be angry with you, and decline to come to your Poojah dinner to drink your champagne, you know. Just think, they mightn't pat you on the back, when you meet them again!"

"It wouldn't break my heart," Nabendu snapped out.

A few days passed. One morning Nabendu was sipping his tea, and glancing at a newspaper. Suddenly a letter signed "X" caught his eye. The writer thanked him profusely for his donation, and declared that the increase of strength the Congress had acquired by having such a man within its fold, was inestimable.

Alas, father Purnendu Sekhar! Was it to increase the strength of the Congress, that you brought this wretch into the world?

Put the cloud of misfortune had its silver lining. That he was not a mere cypher was clear from the fact that the Anglo-Indian community on the one side and the Congress on the other were each waiting patiently, eager to hook him, and land him on their own side. So Nabendu, beaming with pleasure took the paper to his sister-in-law, and showed her the letter. Looking as though she knew nothing about it, Labanya exclaimed in surprise: "Oh, what a pity! Everything has come out! Who bore you such ill-will? Oh, how cruel of him, how wicked of him!"

Nabendu laughed out, saying: "Now, now—don't call him names, Labanya. I forgive him with all my heart, and bless him too."

A couple of days after this, an anti-Congress Anglo-Indian paper reached Nabendu through the post. There was a letter in it, signed "One who knows," and contradicting the above report. "Those who have the pleasure of Babu

Nabendu Sekhar's personal acquaintance," the writer went on, "cannot for a moment believe this absurd libel to be true. For him to turn a Congresswalla is as impossible as it is for the leopard to change his spots. He is a man of genuine worth, and neither a disappointed candidate for Government employ nor a briefless barrister. He is not one of those who, after a brief sojourn in England, return aping our dress and manners, audaciously try to thrust themselves on Anglo-Indian society, and finally go back in dejection. So there is absolutely no reason why Balm Nabendu Sekhar," etc., etc.

Ah, father Purnendu Sekhar! What a reputation you had made with the Europeans before you died!

This letter also was paraded before his sister-in-law, for did it not assert that he was no mean, contemptible scallywag, but a man of real worth?

Labanya exclaimed again in feigned surprise: "Which of your friends wrote it now? Oh, come, is it the Ticket Collector, or the hide merchant, or is it the drum-major of the Fort? "

"You ought to send in a contradiction, I think," said Nilratan.

"Is it necessary?" said Nabendu loftily. Must I contradict every little thing they choose to say against me? "

Labanya filled the room with a deluge of laughter. Nabendu felt a little disconcerted at this, and said: "Why? What's the matter?" She went on laughing, unable to check herself, and her youthful slender form waved to and fro. This torrent of merriment had the effect of overthrowing Nabendu completely, and he said in pitiable accents: "Do you imagine that I am afraid to contradict it?"

"Oh, dear, no," said Labanya; "I was thinking that you haven't yet ceased trying to save that race-course of yours, so full of promise. While there is life, there is hope, you know."

"That's what I am afraid of, you think, do you? Very well, you shall see," said Nabendu desperately, and forthwith sat down to write his contradiction. When he had finished, Labanya and Nilratan read it through, and said: "It isn't strong enough. We must give it them pretty hot, mustn't we?" And they kindly undertook to revise the composition. Thus it ran: "When one connected to us by ties of blood turns our enemy he becomes far more dangerous than any outsider. To the Government of India, the haughty Anglo-Indians are worse enemies than the Russians or the frontier Pathans themselves, they are the impenetrable barrier, forever hindering the growth of any bond of friendship between the Government and people of the country. It is the Congress which has opened up the royal road to a better understanding between the rulers and the ruled, and the Anglo-Indian papers have planted themselves like thorns across the whole breadth of that road," etc., etc.

Nabendu had an inward fear as to the mischief this letter might do, but at the same time he felt elated at the excellence of its composition, which he fondly imagined to be his own. It was duly published, and for some days comments, replies, and rejoinders went on in various newspapers, and the air was full of trumpet-notes, proclaiming the fact that Nabendu had joined the Congress, and the amount of his subscription.

Nabendu, now grown desperate, talked as though he was a patriot of the fiercest type. Labanya laughed inwardly, and said to herself: "Well—well, you have to pass through the ordeal of fire yet."

One morning when Nabendu, before his bath, had finished rubbing oil over his chest, and was trying various devices to reach the inaccessible portions of his back, the bearer brought in a card inscribed with the name of the District Magistrate himself! Good heavens! What would he do? He could not possibly go, and receive the Magistrate Sahib, thus oil-besmeared. He shook and twitched like a koi-fish, ready dressed for the frying pan. He finished his bath in a great hurry, tugged on his clothes somehow, and ran breathlessly to the outer apartments. The bearer said that the Sahib had just left after waiting for a long time. How much of the blame for concocting this drama of invented incidents may be set down to Labanya, and how much to the bearer is a nice problem for ethical mathematics to solve.

Nabendu's heart was convulsed with pain within his breast, like the tail of a lizard just cut off. He moped like an owl all day long.

Labanya banished all traces of inward merriment from her face, and kept on enquiring in anxious tones: "What has happened to you? You are not ill, I hope?"

Nabendu made great efforts to smile, and find a humorous reply. "How can there be," he managed to say, "any illness within your jurisdiction, since you yourself are the Goddess of Health?"

But the smile soon flickered out. His thoughts were: "I subscribed to the Congress fund to begin with, published a nasty letter in a newspaper, and on the top of that, when the Magistrate Sahib himself did me the honour to call on me, I kept him waiting. I wonder what he is thinking of me."

Alas, father Purnendu Sekhar, by an irony of Fate I am made to appear what I am not.

The next morning, Nabendu decked himself in his best clothes, wore his watch and chain, and put a big turban on his head.

"Where are you off to?" enquired his sister-in-law.

"Urgent business," Nabendu replied. Labanya kept quiet.

Arriving at the Magistrate's gate, he took out his card-case.

"You cannot see him now," said the orderly peon icily.

Nabendu took out a couple of rupees from his pocket. The peon at once salaamed him and said: "There are five of us, sir." Immediately Nabendu pulled out a ten-rupee note, and handed it to him.

He was sent for by the Magistrate, who was writing in his dressing-gown and bedroom slippers. Nabendu salaamed him. The Magistrate pointed to a chair with his finger, and without raising his eyes from the paper before him said: "What can I do for you, Babu?"

Fingering his watch-chain nervously, Nabendu said is shaky tones: "Yesterday you were good enough to call at my place, sir—"

The Sahib knitted his brows, and, lifting just one eye from his paper, said: "I called at your place! Babu, what nonsense are you talking?"

"Beg your pardon, sir," faltered out Nabendu. There has been a mistake, some confusion," and wet with perspiration, he tumbled out of the room somehow. And that night, as he lay tossing on his bed, a distant dream-like voice came into his ear with a recurring persistency: "Babu, you are a howling idiot."

On his way home, Nabendu came to the conclusion that the Magistrate denied having called, simply because he was highly offended.

So he explained to Labanya that he had been out purchasing rose-water. No sooner had he uttered the words than half-a-dozen chuprassis wearing the Collectorate badge made their appearance, and after salaaming Nabendu, stood there grinning.

"Have they come to arrest you because you subscribed to the Congress fund?" whispered Labanya with a smile.

The six peons displayed a dozen rows of teeth and said: Bakshish, Babu-Sahib."

From a side room Nilratan came out, and said in an irritated manner: "Bakshish? What for?"

The peons, grinning as before, answered: "The Babu-Sahib went to see the Magistrate, so we have come for bakshish"

"I didn't know," laughed out Labanya, "that the Magistrate was selling rose-water nowadays. Coolness wasn't the special feature of his trade before."

Nabendu in trying to reconcile the story of his purchase with his visit to the Magistrate, uttered some incoherent words, which nobody could make sense of.

Nilratan spoke to the peons: "There has been no occasion for bakshish; you shan't have it."

Nabendu said, feeling very small: "Oh, they are poor men, what's the harm of giving them something?" And he took out a currency note. Nilratan snatched it way from Nabendu's hand, remarking: "There are poorer men in the world, I will give it to them for you."

Nabendu felt greatly distressed that he was not able to appease these ghostly retainers of the angry Siva. When the peons were leaving, with thunder in their eyes, he looked at them languishingly, as much as to say: "You know everything, gentlemen, it is not my fault."

The Congress was to be held at Calcutta this year. Nilratan went down thither with his wife to attend the sittings. Nabendu accompanied them.

As soon as they arrived at Calcutta, the Congress party surrounded Nabendu, and their delight and enthusiasm knew no bounds. They cheered him, honoured him, and extolled him up to the skies. Everybody said that, unless leading men like Nabendu devoted themselves to the Cause, there was no hope for the country. Nabendu was disposed to agree with them, and emerged out of the chaos of mistake and confusion as a leader of the country. When he entered the Congress Pavilion on the first day, everybody stood up, and shouted " Hip, hip, hurrah," in a loud outlandish voice, hearing which our Motherland reddened with shame to the root of her ears.

In due time the Queen's birthday came, and Nabendu's name was not found in the list of Rai Bahadurs.

He received an invitation from Labanya for that evening. When he arrived there, Labanya with great pomp and ceremony presented him with a robe of honour, and with her own hand put a mark of red sandal paste on the middle of his forehead. Each of the other sisters threw round his neck a garland of flowers woven by herself. Decked in a pink Sari and dazzling jewels, his wife Arunlekha was waiting in a side room, her face lit up with smiles and blushes. Her sisters rushed to her, and, placing another garland in her hand, insisted that she also should come, and do her part in the ceremony, but she would not listen to it; and that principal garland, cherishing a desire for Nabendu's neck, waited patiently for the still secrecy of midnight.

The sisters said to Nabendu : "To-day we crown thee King. Such honour will not be done to anybody else in Hindoostan."

Whether Nabendu derived any consolation from this, he alone can tell; but we greatly doubt it. We believe, in fact, that he will become a Rai Bahadur before he has done, and the Englishman and the Pioneer will write heart-rending articles lamenting his demise at the proper time. So, in the meanwhile, Three Cheers for Babu Purnendu Sekhar! Hip, hip, hurrah – H ip, hip, hurrah - Hip, hip, hurrah.

Once There Was A King

"Once upon a time there was a king."

When we were children there was no need to know who the king in the fairy story was. It didn't matter whether he was called Shiladitya or Shaliban, whether he lived at Kashi or Kanauj. The thing that made a seven-year-old boy's heart go thump, thump with delight was this one sovereign truth; this reality of all realities: "Once there was a king."

But the readers of this modern age are far more exact and exacting. When they hear such an opening to a story, they are at once critical and suspicious. They apply the searchlight of science to its legendary haze and ask: "Which king?"

The story-tellers have become more precise in their turn. They are no longer content with the old indefinite, "There was a king," but assume instead a look of profound learning, and begin: "Once there was a king named Ajatasatru,"

The modern reader's curiosity, however, is not so easily satisfied. He blinks at the author through his scientific spectacles, and asks again: "Which Ajatasatru?"

"Every schoolboy knows," the author proceeds, "that there were three Ajatasatrus. The first was born in the twentieth century B.C., and died at the tender age of two years and eight months, I deeply regret that it is impossible to find, from any trustworthy source, a detailed account of his reign. The second Ajatasatru is better known to historians. If you refer to the new Encyclopedia of History. . . ."

By this time the modem reader's suspicions are dissolved. He feels he may safely trust his author. He says to himself: "Now we shall have a story that is both improving and instructive."

Ah! how we all love to be deluded! We have a secret dread of being thought ignorant. And we end by being ignorant after all, only we have done it in a long and roundabout way.

There is an English proverb; "Ask me no questions, and I will tell you no lies." The boy of seven who is listening to a fairy story understands that perfectly well; he withholds his questions, while the story is being told. So the pure and beautiful falsehood of it all remains naked and innocent as a babe; transparent as truth itself; limpid as afresh bubbling spring. But the ponderous and learned lie of our moderns has to keep its true character draped and veiled. And if there is discovered anywhere the least little peep-hole of deception, the reader turns away with a prudish disgust, and the author is discredited.

When we were young, we understood all sweet things; and we could detect the sweets of a fairy story by an unerring science of our own. We never cared for such useless things as knowledge. We only cared for truth. And our unsophisticated little hearts knew well where the Crystal Palace of Truth lay and how to reach it. But to-day we are expected to write pages of facts, while the truth is simply this:

"There was a king."

I remember vividly that evening in Calcutta when the fairy story began. The rain and the storm had been incessant. The whole of the city was flooded. The water was knee-deep in our lane. I had a straining hope, which was almost a certainty, that my tutor would be prevented from coming that evening. I sat on the stool in the far corner of the veranda looking down the lane, with a heart beating faster and faster. Every minute I kept my eye on the rain, and when it began to grow less I prayed with all my might; "Please, God, send some more rain till half- past seven is over." For I was quite ready to believe that there was no other need for rain except to protect one helpless boy one evening in one corner of Calcutta from the deadly clutches of his tutor.

If not in answer to my prayer, at any rate according to some grosser law of physical nature, the rain did not give up.

But, alas ! nor did my teacher.

Exactly to the minute, in the bend of the lane, I saw his approaching umbrella. The great bubble of hope burst in my breast, and my heart collapsed. Truly, if there is a punishment to fit the crime after death, then my tutor will be born again as me, and I shall be born as my tutor.

As soon as I saw his umbrella I ran as hard as I could to my mother's room. My mother and my grandmother were sitting opposite one another playing cards by the light of a lamp. I ran into the room, and flung myself on the bed beside my mother, and said:

"Mother dear, the tutor has come, and I have such a bad headache; couldn't I have no lessons today?"

I hope no child of immature age will be allowed to read this story, and I sincerely trust it will not be used in text-books or primers for schools. For what I did was dreadfully bad, and I received no punishment whatever. On the contrary, my wickedness was crowned with success.

My mother said to me: "All right," and turning to the servant added: "Tell the tutor that he can go back home."

It was perfectly plain that she didn't think my illness very serious, as she went on with her game as before, and took no further notice. And I also, burying my head in the pillow, laughed to my heart's content. We perfectly understood one another, my mother and I.

But everyone must know how hard it is for a boy of seven years old to keep up the illusion of illness for a long time. After about a minute I got hold of Grandmother, and said: "Grannie, do tell me a story."

I had to ask this many times. Grannie and Mother went on playing cards, and took no notice. At last Mother said to me: "Child, don't bother. Wait till we've finished our game." But I persisted: "Grannie, do tell me a story." I told Mother she could finish her game to-morrow, but she must let Grannie tell me a story there and then.

At last Mother threw down the cards and said: "You had better do what he wants. I can't manage him." Perhaps she had it in her mind that she would have no tiresome tutor on the morrow, while I should be obliged to be back to those stupid lessons.

As soon as ever Mother had given way, I rushed at Grannie. I got hold of her hand, and, dancing with delight, dragged her inside my mosquito curtain on to the bed. I clutched hold of the bolster with both hands in my excitement, and jumped up and down with joy, and when I had got a little quieter, said: "Now, Grannie, let' s have the story!"

Grannie went on: "And the king had a queen." That was good to begin with. He had only one.

It is usual for kings in fairy stories to be extravagant in queens. And whenever we hear that there are two queens, our hearts begin to sink. One is sure to be unhappy. But in Grannie's story that danger was past. He had only one queen.

We next hear that the king had not got any son. At the age of seven I didn't think there was any need to bother if a man had had no son. He might only have been in the way. Nor are we greatly excited when we hear that the king has gone away into the forest to practise austerities in order to get a son. There was only one thing that would have made me go into the forest, and that was to get away from my tutor!

But the king left behind with his queen a small girl, who grew up into a beautiful princess.

Twelve years pass away, and the king goes on practising austerities, and never thinks all this while of his beautiful daughter. The princess has reached the full bloom of her youth. The age of marriage has passed, but the king does not return. And the queen pines away with grief and cries : "Is my golden daughter destined to die unmarried? Ah me! What a fate is mine."

Then the queen sent men to the king to entreat him earnestly to come back for a single night and take one meal in the palace. And the king consented.

The queen cooked with her own hand, and with the greatest care, sixty- four dishes, and made a seat for him of sandal-wood, and arranged the food in plates of gold and cups of silver. The princess stood behind with the peacock-tail fan in her hand. The king, after twelve years' absence, came into the house, and the princess waved the fan, lighting up all the room with her beauty. The king looked in his daughter's face, and forgot to take his food.

At last he asked his queen: "Pray, who is this girl whose beauty shines as the gold image of the goddess? Whose daughter is she?"

The queen beat her forehead, and cried: "Ah, how evil is my fate ! Do you not know your own daughter?"

The king was struck with amazement. He said at last; "My tiny daughter has grown to be a woman."

"What else?" the queen said with a sigh. "Do you not know that twelve years have passed by?"

"But why did you not give her in marriage?" asked the king.

"You were away," the queen said. "And how could I find her a suitable husband?"

The king became vehement with excitement. "The first man I see to-morrow," he said, "when I come out of the palace shall marry her."

The princess went on waving her fan of peacock feathers, and the king finished his meal.

The next morning, as the king came out of his palace, he saw the son of a Brahman gathering sticks in the forest outside the palace gates. His age was about seven or eight.

The king said: "I will marry my daughter to him."

Who can interfere with a king's command? At once the boy was called, and the marriage garlands were exchanged between him and the princess.

At this point I came up close to my wise Grannie and asked her eagerly: "What then?"

In the bottom of my heart there was a devout wish to substitute myself for that fortunate wood-gatherer of seven years old. The night was resonant with the patter of rain. The earthen lamp by my bedside was burning low. My grandmother's voice droned on as she told the story. And all these things served to create in a corner of my credulous heart the belief that I had been gathering sticks in the dawn of some indefinite time in the kingdom of some unknown king, and in a moment garlands had been exchanged between me and the princess, beautiful as the Goddess of Grace. She had a gold band on her hair and gold earrings in her ears. She bad a necklace and bracelets of gold, and a golden waist-chain round her waist, and a pair of golden anklets tinkled above her feet.

If my grandmother were an author how many explanations she would have to offer for this little story! First of all, everyone would ask why the king remained twelve years in the forest? Secondly, why should the king's daughter remain unmarried all that while? This would be regarded as absurd.

Even if she could have got so far without a quarrel, still there would have been a great hue and cry about the marriage itself. First, it never happened. Secondly, how could there be a marriage between a princess of the Warrior Caste and a boy of the priestly Brahman Caste? Her readers would have imagined at once that the writer was preaching against our social customs in an underhand way. And they would write letters to the papers.

So I pray with all my heart that my grandmother may be born a grandmother again, and not through some cursed fate take birth as her luckless grandson.

So with a throb of joy and delight, I asked Grannie: "What then?"

Grannie went on: Then the princess took her little husband away in great distress, and built a large palace with seven wings, and began to cherish her husband with great care.

I jumped up and down in my bed and clutched at the bolster more tightly than ever and said: "What then?"

Grannie continued : The little boy went to school and learnt many lessons from his teachers, and as he grew up his class-fellows began to ask him: "Who is that beautiful lady who lives with you in the palace with the seven wings? " The Brahman's son was eager to know who she was. He could only remember how one day he had been gathering sticks, and a great disturbance arose. But all that was so long ago, that he had no clear recollection.

Four or five years passed in this way. His companions always asked him: "Who is that beautiful lady in the palace with the seven wings?" And the Brahman's son would come back from school and sadly tell the princess: "My school companions always ask me who is that beautiful lady in the palace with the seven wings, and I can give them no reply. Tell me, oh, tell me, who you are!"

The princess said: "Let it pass to-day. I will tell you some other day." And every day the Brahman's son would ask; "Who are you?" and the princess would reply: "Let it pass to-day. I will tell you some other day." In this manner four or five more years passed away.

At last the Brahman's son became very impatient, and said: "If you do not tell me to-day who you are, O beautiful lady, I will leave this palace with the seven wings." Then the princess said: "I will certainly tell you to-morrow."

Next day the Brahman's son, as soon as he came home from school, said: "Now, tell me who you are." The princess said: "To-night I will tell you after supper, when you are in bed."

The Brahman's son said: "Very well"; and he began to count the hours in expectation of the night. And the princess, on her side, spread white flowers over the golden bed, and lighted a gold lamp with fragrant oil, and adorned her hair, and dressed herself in a beautiful robe of blue, and began to count the hours in expectation of the night.

That evening when her husband, the Brahman's son, had finished his meal, too excited almost to eat, and had gone to the golden bed in the bed- chamber strewn with flowers, he said to himself: "To-night I shall surely know who this beautiful lady is in the palace with the seven wings."

The princess took for her the food that was left over by her husband, and slowly entered the bed-chamber. She had to answer that night the question, which was the beautiful lady who lived in the palace with the seven wings. And as she went up to the bed to tell him she found a serpent had crept out of the flowers and had bitten the Brahman's son. Her boy-husband was lying on the bed of flowers, with face pale in death.

My heart suddenly ceased to throb, and I asked with choking voice: "What then?"

Grannie said; "Then . . ."

But what is the use of going on any further with the story? It would only lead on to what was more and more impossible. The boy of seven did not know that, if there were some "What then? " after death, no grandmother of a grandmother could tell us all about it.

But the child's faith never admits defeat, and it would snatch at the mantle of death itself to turn him back. It would be outrageous for him to think that such a story of one teacherless evening could so suddenly come to a stop. Therefore the grandmother had to call back her story from the ever-shut chamber of the great End, but she does it so simply: it is merely by floating the dead body on a banana stem on the river, and having some incantations read by a magician. But in that rainy night and in the dim light of a lamp death loses all its horror in the mind of the boy, and seems nothing more than a deep slumber of a single night. When the story ends the tired eyelids are weighed down with sleep. Thus it is that we send the little body of the child floating on the back of sleep over the still water of time, and then in the morning read a few verses of incantation to restore him to the world of life and light.

My Lord, The Baby

I

Raicharan was twelve years old when he came as a servant to his master's house. He belonged to the same caste as his master, and was given his master's little son to nurse. As time went on the boy left Raicharan's arms to go to school. From school he went on to college, and after college he entered the judicial service. Always, until he married, Raicharan was his sole attendant.

But, when a mistress came into the house, Raicharan found two masters instead of one. All his former influence passed to the new mistress. This was compensated for by a fresh arrival. Anukul had a son born to him, and Raicharan by his unsparing attentions soon got a complete hold over the child. He used to toss him up in his arms, call to him in absurd baby language, put his face close to the baby's and draw it away again with a grin.

Presently the child was able to crawl and cross the doorway. When Raicharan went to catch him, he would scream with mischievous laughter and make for safety. Raicharan was amazed at the profound skill and exact judgment the baby showed when pursued. He would say to his mistress with a look of awe and mystery: "Your son will be a judge some day."

New wonders came in their turn. When the baby began to toddle, that was to Raicharan an epoch in human history. When he called his father Ba-ba and his mother Ma-ma and Raicharan Chan-na, then Raicharan's ecstasy knew no bounds. He went out to tell the news to all the world.

After a while Raicharan was asked to show his ingenuity in other ways. He had, for instance, to play the part of a horse, holding the reins between his teeth and prancing with his feet. He had also to wrestle with his little charge, and if he could not, by a wrestler's trick, fall on his back defeated at the end, a great outcry was certain.

About this time Anukul was transferred to a district on the banks of the Padma. On his way through Calcutta he bought his son a little go-cart. He bought him also a yellow satin waistcoat, a gold-laced cap, and some gold bracelets and anklets. Raicharan was wont to take these out, and put them on his little charge with ceremonial pride, whenever they went for a walk.

Then came the rainy season, and day after day the rain poured down in torrents. The hungry river, like an enormous serpent, swallowed down terraces, villages, cornfields, and covered with its flood the tall grasses and wild casuarinas on the sand-banks. From time to time there was a deep thud, as the river-banks crumbled. The unceasing roar of the rain current could be beard from far away. Masses of foam, carried swiftly past, proved to the eye the swiftness of the stream.

One afternoon the rain cleared. It was cloudy, but cool and bright. Raicharan's little despot did not want to stay in on such a fine afternoon. His lordship climbed into the go-cart. Raicharan, between the shafts, dragged him slowly along till he reached the rice-fields on the banks of the river. There was no one in the fields, and no boat on the stream. Across the water, on the farther side, the clouds were rifted in the west. The silent ceremonial of the setting sun was revealed in all its glowing splendour. In the midst of that stillness the child, all of a sudden, pointed with his finger in front of him and cried: "Chan-nal Pitty fow."

Close by on a mud-flat stood a large Kadamba tree in full flower. My lord, the baby, looked at it with greedy eyes, and Raicharan knew his meaning. Only a short time before he had made, out of these very flower balls, a small go-cart; and the child had been so entirely happy dragging it about with a string, that for the whole day Raicharan was not made to put on the reins at all. He was promoted from a horse into a groom.

But Raicharan had no wish that evening to go splashing knee-deep through the mud to reach the flowers. So he quickly pointed his finger in the opposite direction, calling out: "Oh, look, baby, look! Look at the bird." And with all sorts of curious noises he pushed the go-cart rapidly away from the tree.

But a child, destined to be a judge, cannot be put off so easily. And besides, there was at the time nothing to attract his eyes. And you cannot keep up for ever the pretence of an imaginary bird.

The little Master's mind was made up, and Raicharan was at his wits' end. "Very well, baby," he said at last, "you sit still in the cart, and I'll go and get you the pretty flower. Only mind you don't go near the water."

As he said this, he made his legs bare to the knee, and waded through the oozing mud towards the tree.

The moment Raicharan had gone, his little Master went off at racing speed to the forbidden water. The baby saw the river rushing by, splashing and gurgling as it went. It seemed as though the disobedient wavelets themselves were running away from some greater Raicharan with the laughter of a thousand children. At the sight of their mischief, the heart of the human child grew excited and restless. He got down stealthily from the go-cart and toddled off towards the river. On his way he picked up a small stick, and leant over the bank of the stream pretending to fish. The mischievous fairies of the river with their mysterious voices seemed inviting him into their play-house.

Raicharan had plucked a handful of flowers from the tree, and was carrying them back in the end of his cloth, with his face wreathed in smiles. But when he reached the go-cart, there was no one there. He looked on all sides and there was no one there. He looked back at the cart and there was no one there.

In that first terrible moment his blood froze within him. Before his eyes the whole universe swam round like a dark mist. From the depth of his broken heart he gave one piercing cry; "Master, Master, little Master."

But no voice answered "Chan-na." No child laughed mischievously back; no scream of baby delight welcomed his return. Only the river ran on, with its splashing, gurgling noise as before, as though it knew nothing at all, and had no time to attend to such a tiny human event as the death of a child.

As the evening passed by Raicharan's mistress became very anxious. She sent men out on all sides to search. They went with lanterns in their hands, and reached at last the banks of the Padma. There they found Raicharan rushing up and down the fields, like a stormy wind, shouting the cry of despair: "Master, Master, little Master!"

When they got Raicharan home at last, he fell prostrate at his mistress's feet. They shook him, and questioned him, and asked him repeatedly where he had left the child; but all he could say was, that he knew nothing.

Though everyone held the opinion that the Padma had swallowed the child, there was a lurking doubt left in the mind. For a band of gipsies had been noticed outside the village that afternoon, and some suspicion rested on them. The mother went so far in her wild grief as to think it possible that Raicharan himself had stolen the child. She called him aside with piteous entreaty and said: "Raicharan, give me back my baby. Oh ! give me back my child. Take from me any money you ask, but give me back my child!"

Raicharan only beat his forehead in reply. His mistress ordered him out of the house.

Artukul tried to reason his wife out of this wholly unjust suspicion: "Why on earth," he said, "should he commit such a crime as that?"

The mother only replied: "The baby had gold ornaments on his body. Who knows?"

It was impossible to reason with her after that.

II

Raicharan went back to his own village. Up to this time he had had no son, and there was no hope that any child would now be born to him. But it came about before the end of a year that his wife gave birth to a son and died.

All overwhelming resentment at first grew up in Raicharan's heart at the sight of this new baby. At the back of his mind was resentful suspicion that it had come as a usurper in place of the little Master. He also thought it would be a grave offence to be happy with a son of his own after what had happened to his master's little child. Indeed, if it had not been for a widowed sister, who mothered the new baby, it would not have lived long.

But a change gradually came over Raicharan's mind. A wonderful thing happened. This new baby in turn began to crawl about, and cross the doorway with mischief in its face. It also showed an amusing cleverness in making its escape to safety. Its voice, its sounds of laughter and tears, its gestures, were those of the little Master. On some days, when Raicharan listened to its crying, his heart suddenly began thumping wildly against his ribs, and it seemed to him that his former little Master was crying somewhere in the unknown land of death because he had lost his Chan-na.

Phailna (for that was the name Raicharan's sister gave to the new baby) soon began to talk. It learnt to say Ba-ba and Ma-ma with a baby accent. When Raicharan heard those familiar sounds the mystery suddenly became clear. The little Master could not cast off the spell of his Chan-na, and therefore he had been reborn in his own house.

The arguments in favour of this were, to Raicharan, altogether beyond dispute:

(i.) The new baby was born soon after his little master's death.

(ii.) His wife could never have accumulated such merit as to give birth to a son in middle age.

(iii.) The new baby walked with a toddle and called out Ba-ba and Ma- ma. There was no sign lacking which marked out the future judge.

Then suddenly Raicharan remembered that terrible accusation of the mother. "Ah," he said to himself with amazement, "the mother's heart was right. She knew I had stolen her child." When once he had come to this conclusion, he was filled with remorse for his past neglect. He now gave himself over, body and soul, to the new baby, and became its devoted attendant. He began to bring it up, as if it were the son of a rich man. He bought a go-cart, a yellow satin waistcoat, and a gold- embroidered cap. He melted down the ornaments of his dead wife, and made gold bangles and anklets. He refused to let the little child play with any one of the neighbourhood, and became himself its sole companion day and night. As the baby grew up to boyhood, he was so petted and spoilt and clad in such finery that the village children would call him "Your Lordship," and jeer at him; and older people regarded Raicharan as unaccountably crazy about the child.

At last the time came for the boy to go to school. Raicharan sold his small piece of land, and went to Calcutta. There he got employment with great difficulty as a servant, and sent Phailna to school. He spared no pains to give him the best education, the best clothes, the best food. Meanwhile he lived himself on a mere handful of rice, and would say in secret: "Ah! my little Master, my dear little Master, you loved me so much that you came back to my house. You shall never suffer from any neglect of mine."

Twelve years passed away in this manner. The boy was able to read and write well. He was bright and healthy and good-looking. He paid a great deal of attention to his personal appearance, and was specially careful in parting his hair. He was inclined to extravagance and finery, and spent money freely. He could never quite look on Raicharan as a father, because, though fatherly in affection, he had the manner of a servant. A further fault was this, that Raicharan kept secret from every one that himself was the father of the child.

The students of the hostel, where Phailna was a boarder, were greatly amused by Raicharan's country manners, and I have to confess that behind his father's back Phailna joined in their fun. But, in the bottom of their hearts, all the students loved the innocent and tender-hearted old man, and Phailna was very fond of him also. But, as I have said before, he loved him with a kind of condescension.

Raicharan grew older and older, and his employer was continually finding fault with him for his incompetent work. He had been starving himself for the boy's sake. So he had grown physically weak, and no longer up to his work. He would forget things, and his mind became dull and stupid. But his employer expected a full servant's work out of him, and would not brook excuses. The money that Raicharan had brought with him from the sale of his land was exhausted. The boy was continually grumbling about his clothes, and asking for more money.

Raicharan made up his mind. He gave up the situation where he was working as a servant, and left some money with Phailna and said: "I have some business to do at home in my village, and shall be back soon."

He went off at once to Baraset where Anukul was magistrate. Anukul's wife was still broken down with grief. She had had no other child.

One day Anukul was resting after a long and weary day in court. His wife was buying, at an exorbitant price, a herb from a mendicant quack, which was said to ensure the birth of a child. A voice of greeting was heard in the courtyard. Anukul went out to see who was there. It was Raicharan. Anukul's heart was softened when he saw his old servant. He asked him many questions, and offered to take him back into service.

Raicharan smiled faintly, and said in reply; "I want to make obeisance to my mistress."

Anukul went with Raicharan into the house, where the mistress did not receive him as warmly as his old master. Raicharan took no notice of this, but folded his hands, and said: "It was not the Padma that stole your baby. It was I."

Anukul exclaimed: "Great God! Eh! What! Where is he ? "Raicharan replied: "He is with me, I will bring him the day after to-morrow."

It was Sunday. There was no magistrate's court sitting. Both husband and wife were looking expectantly along the road, waiting from early morning for Raicharan's appearance. At ten o'clock he came, leading Phailna by the hand.

Anukul's wife, without a question, took the boy into her lap, and was wild with excitement, sometimes laughing, sometimes weeping, touching him, kissing his hair and his forehead, and gazing into his face with hungry, eager eyes. The boy was very good-looking and dressed like a gentleman's son. The heart of Anukul brimmed over with a sudden rush of affection.

Nevertheless the magistrate in him asked: "Have you any proofs? "Raicharan said: "How could there be any proof of such a deed? God alone knows that I stole your boy, and no one else in the world."

When Anukul saw how eagerly his wife was clinging to the boy, he realised the futility of asking for proofs. It would be wiser to believe. And then, where could an old man like Raicharan get such a boy from? And why should his faithful servant deceive him for nothing?

"But," he added severely, "Raicharan, you must not stay here."

"Where shall I go, Master?" said Raicharan, in a choking voice, folding his hands; "I am old. Who will take in an old man as a servant?"

The mistress said: "Let him stay. My child will be pleased. I forgive him."

But Anukul's magisterial conscience would not allow him. "No," he said, "he cannot be forgiven for what he has done."

Raicharan bowed to the ground, and clasped Anukul's feet. "Master," he cried, "let me stay. It was not I who did it. It was God."

Anukul's conscience was worse stricken than ever, when Raicharan tried to put the blame on God's shoulders.

"No," he said, "I could not allow it. I cannot trust you any more. You have done an act of treachery."

Raicharan rose to his feet and said: "It was not I who did it."

"Who was it then?" asked Anukul.

Raicharan replied: "It was my fate."

But no educated man could take this for an excuse. Anukul remained obdurate.

When Phailna saw that he was the wealthy magistrate's son, and not Raicharan's, be was angry at first, thinking that he had been cheated all this time of his birthright. But seeing Raicharan in distress, he generously said to his father: "Father, forgive him. Even if you don't let him live with us, let him have a small monthly pension."

After hearing this, Raicharan did not utter another word. He looked for the last time on the face of his son; he made obeisance to his old master and mistress. Then he went out, and was mingled with the numberless people of the world.

At the end of the month Anukul sent him some money to his village. But the money came back. There was no one there of the name of Raicharan.

The Babus Of NayanJore
I

Once upon a time the Babus of Nayanjore were famous landholders. They were noted for their princely extravagance. They would tear off the rough border of their Dacca muslin, because it rubbed against their skin. They could spend many thousands of rupees over the wedding of a kitten. On a certain grand occasion it is alleged that in order to turn night into day they lighted numberless lamps and showered silver threads from the sky to imitate sunlight. Those were the days before the flood. The flood came. The line of succession among these old-world Babus, with their lordly habits, could not continue for long. Like a lamp with too many wicks burning, the oil flared away quickly, and the light went out.

Kailas Babu, our neighbour, is the last relic of this extinct magnificence. Before he grew up, his family had very nearly reached its lowest ebb. When his father died, there was one dazzling outburst of funeral extravagance, and then insolvency. The property was sold to liquidate the debt. What little ready money was left over was altogether insufficient to keep up the past ancestral splendours.

Kailas Babu left Nayanjore, and came to Calcutta. His son did not remain long in this world of faded glory. He died, leaving behind him an only daughter.

In Calcutta we are Kailas Baba's neighbours. Curiously enough our own family history is just the opposite to his. My father got his money by his own exertions, and prided himself on never spending a penny more than was needed. His clothes were those of a working man, and his hands also. He never had any inclination to earn the title of Baba by extravagant display, and I myself his only son, owe him gratitude for that. He gave me the very best education, and I was able to make my way in the world. I am not ashamed of the fact that I am a self-made man. Crisp bank-notes in my safe are dearer to me than a long pedigree in an empty family chest.

I believe this was why I disliked seeing Kailas Baba drawing his heavy cheques on the public credit from the bankrupt bank of his ancient Babu reputation I used to fancy that he looked down on me, because my father had earned money with his own hands.

I ought to have noticed that no one showed any vexation towards Kailas Babu except myself. Indeed it would have been difficult to find an old man who did less harm than he. He was always ready with his kindly little acts of courtesy in times of sorrow and joy. He would join in all the ceremonies and religious observances of his neighbours. His familiar smile would greet young and old alike. His politeness in asking details about domestic affairs was untiring. The friends who met him in the street were perforce ready to be button-holed, while a long string of questions of this kind followed one another from his lips:

"My dear friend, I am delighted to see you. Are quite well? How is Shashi? and Dada—is he all right? Do you know, I've only just heard that Madhu's son has got fever. How is he? Have you heard? And Hari Charan Babu—I've not seen him for a long time, I hope he is not ill. What's the matter with Rakkhal? And, er - er, how are the ladies of your family?"

Kailas Balm was spotlessly neat in his dress on all occasions, though his supply of clothes was sorely limited. Every day he used to air his shirts and vests and coats and trousers carefully, and put them out in the sun, along with his bed-quilt, his pillowcase, and the small carpet on which he always sat. After airing them he would shake them, and brush them, and put them on the rock. His little bits of furniture made his small room decent, and hinted that there was more in reserve if needed. Very often, for want of a servant, he would shut up his house for a while. Then he would iron out his shirts and linen with his own hands, and do other little menial tasks. After this he would open his door and receive his friends again.

Though Kailas Balm, as I have said, had lost all his landed property, he had still same family heirlooms left. There was a silver cruet for sprinkling scented water, a filigree box for otto-of-roses, a small gold salver, a costly ancient shawl, and the old-fashioned ceremonial dress and ancestral turban. These he had rescued with the greatest difficulty from the money-lenders' clutches. On every suitable occasion he would bring them out in state, and thus try to save the world-famed dignity of the Babus of Nayanjore. At heart the most modest of men, in his daily speech he regarded it as a sacred duty, owed to his rank, to give free play to his family pride. His friends would encourage this trait in his character with kindly good-humour, and it gave them great amusement.

The neighbourhood soon learnt to call him their Thakur Dada (Grandfather). They would flock to his house, and sit with him for hours together. To prevent his incurring any expense, one or other of his friends would bring him tobacco, and say: "Thakur Dada, this morning some tobacco was sent to me from Gaya. Do take it, and see how you like it"

Thakur Dada would take it, and say it was excellent. He would then go on to tell of a certain exquisite tobacco which they once smoked in the old days at Nayanjore at the cost of a guinea an ounce.

"I wonder," he used to say, "I wonder if anyone would like to try it now. I have some left, and can get it at once"

Everyone knew, that, if they asked for it, then somehow or other the key of the cupboard would he missing; or else Ganesh, his old family servant, had put it away somewhere.

"You never can be sure," he would add," where things go to when servants are about. Now, this Ganesh of mine,- I can't tell you what a fool he is, but I haven't the heart to dismiss him."

Ganesh, for the credit of the family, was quite ready to bear all the blame without a word.

One of the company usually said at this point: "Never mind, Thakur Dada. Please don't trouble to look for it. This tobacco we're smoking will do quite well. The other would be too strong."

Then Thakur Dada would be relieved, and settle down again, and the talk would go on.

When his guests got up to go away, Thakur Dada would accompany them to the door, and say to them on the door-step: "Oh, by the way, when are you all coming to dine with me?"

One or other of us would answer: "Not just yet, Thakur Dada, not just yet. We'll fix a day later."

"Quite right," he would answer. "Quite right. We had much better wait till the rains come. It's too hot now. And a grand rich dinner such as I should want to give you would upset us in weather like this."

But when the rains did come, every one careful not to remind him of his promise. If the subject was brought up, some friend would suggest gently that it was very inconvenient to get about when the rains were so severe, that it would be much better to wait till they were over. And so the game went on.

His poor lodging was much too small for his position, and we used to condole with him about it. His friends would assure him they quite understood his difficulties: it was next to impossible to get a decent house in Calcutta. Indeed, they had all been looking out for years for a house to suit him, but, I need hardly add, no friend had been foolish enough to find one. Thakur Dada used to say, after a long sigh of resignation: "Well, well, I suppose I shall have to put up with this house after all." Then he would add with a genial smile: "But, you know, I could never bear to he away from my friends. I must be near you. That really compensates for everything."

Somehow I felt all this very deeply indeed. I suppose the real reason was, that when a man is young stupidity appears to him the worst of crimes. Kailas Babu was not really stupid. In ordinary business matters everyone was ready to consult him.

But with regard to Nayanjore his utterances were certainly void of common sense. Because, out of amused affection for him, no one contradicted his impossible statements, he refused to keep them in bounds. When people recounted in his hearing the glorious history of Nayanjore with absurd exaggerations he would accept all they said with the utmost gravity, and never doubted, even in his dreams, that anyone could disbelieve it.

II

When I sit down and try to analyse the thoughts and feelings that I had towards Kailas Babu I see that there was a still deeper reason for my dislike. I will now explain.

Though I am the son of a rich man, and might have wasted time at college, my industry was such that I took my M.A. degree in Calcutta University when quite young. My moral character was flawless. In addition, my outward appearance was so handsome, that if I were to call myself beautiful, it might be thought a mark of self-estimation, but could not be considered an untruth.

There could be no question that among the young men of Bengal I was regarded by parents generally as a very eligible match. I was myself quite clear on the point, and had determined to obtain my full value in the marriage market. When I pictured my choice, I had before my mind's eye a wealthy father's only daughter, extremely beautiful and highly educated. Proposals came pouring in to me from far and near; large sums in cash were offered. I weighed these offers with rigid impartiality, in the delicate scales of my own estimation. But there was no one fit to be my partner. I became convinced, with the poet Bhabavuti, that

In this worlds endless time and boundless space One may be born at last to match my sovereign grace.

But in this puny modern age, and this contracted space of modern Bengal, it was doubtful if the peerless creature existed as yet.

Meanwhile my praises were sung in many tunes, and in different metres, by designing parents.

Whether I was pleased with their daughters or not, this worship which they offered was never unpleasing. I used to regard it as my proper due, because I was so good. We are told that when the gods withhold their boons from mortals they still expect their worshippers to pay them fervent honour, and are angry if it is withheld. I had that divine expectance strongly developed in myself.

I have already mentioned that Thakur Dada had an only grand-daughter. I had seen her many times, but had never mistaken her for beautiful. No thought had ever entered my mind that she would be a possible partner for myself. All the same, it seemed quite certain to me that some day ox other Kailas Babu would offer her, with all due worship, as an oblation at my shrine. Indeed-this was the secret of my dislike-I was thoroughly annoyed that he had not done it already.

I heard he had told his friends that the Babus of Nayanjore never craved a boon. Even if the girl remained unmarried, he would not break the family tradition. It was this arrogance of his that made me angry. My indignation smouldered for some time. But I remained perfectly silent, and bore it with the utmost patience, because I was so good.

As lightning accompanies thunder, so in my character a flash of humour was mingled with the mutterings of my wrath. It was, of course, impossible for me to punish the old man merely to give vent to my rage; and for a long time I did nothing at all. But suddenly one day such an amusing plan came into my head, that I could not resist the temptation of carrying it into effect.

I have already said that many of Kailas Babu's friends used to flatter the old man's vanity to the full. One, who was a retired Government servant, had told him that whenever he saw the Chota Lord Sahib he always asked for the latest news about the Babus of Nayanjore, and the Chota Lard had been heard to say that in all Bengal the only really respectable families were those of the Maharaja of Burdwan and the Babus of Nayanjore. When this monstrous falsehood was told to Kailas Balm he was extremely gratified, and often repeated the story. And wherever after that he met this Government servant in company he would ask, along with other questions:

"Oh! Er, by the way, how is the Chota Lord Sahib? Quite well, did you say? Ah, yes, I am so delighted to hear it I And the dear Mem Sahib, is she quite well too? Ah, yes! and the little children-are they quite well also? Ah, yes I that's very goad news! Be sure and give them my compliments when you see them."

Kailas Balm would constantly express his intention of going some day and paying a visit to the Sahib.

But it may be taken for granted that many Chota Lords and Burro Lords also would come and go, and much water would pass down the Hoogly, before the family coach of Nayanjore would be furnished up to pay a visit to Government House.

One day I took Kailas Babu aside, and told him in a whisper: "Thakur Dada, I was at the Levee yesterday, and the Chota Lord happened to mention the Babes of Nayanjore. I told him that Kailas Balm had come to town. Do you know, he was terribly hurt because you hadn't called. He told me he was going to put etiquette on one side, and pay you a private visit himself this very afternoon."

Anybody else could have seen through this plot of mine in a moment. And, if it had been directed against another person, Kailas Balm would have understood the joke. But after all he had heard from his friend the Government servant, and after all his own exaggerations, a visit from the Lieutenant-Governor seemed the most natural thing in the world. He became highly nervous and excited at my news. Each detail of the coming visit exercised him greatly -most of all his own ignorance of English. How on earth was that difficulty to be met? I told him there was no difficulty at all: it was aristocratic not to know English: and, besides, the Lieutenant-Governor always brought an interpreter with him, and he had expressly mentioned that this visit was to be private.

About mid-day, when most of our neighbours are at work, and the rest are asleep, a carriage and pair stopped before the lodging of Kailas Babu. Two flunkeys in livery came up the stairs, and announced in a loud voice, "The Chota Lord Sahib hoe arrived." Kailas Babu was ready, waiting for him, in his old-fashioned ceremonial robes and ancestral turban, and Ganesh was by his side, dressed in his master's best suit of clothes for the occasion. When the Chota Lord Sahib was announced, Kailas Balm ran panting and puffing and trembling to the door, and led in a friend of mine, in disguise, with repeated salaams, bowing low at each step, and walking backward as best he could. He had his old family shawl spread over a hard wooden chair, and he asked the Lord Sahib to be seated. He then made a high. flown speech in Urdu, the ancient Court language of the Sahibs, and presented on the golden salver a string of gold mohurs, the last relics of his broken fortune. The old family servant Ganesh, with an expression of awe bordering on terror, stood behind with the scent-sprinkler, drenching the Lord Sahib, touching him gingerly from time to time with the otto-of-roses from the filigree box.

Kailas Babu repeatedly expressed his regret at not being able to receive His Honour Bahadur with all the ancestral magnificence of his own family estate at Nayanjore. There he could have welcomed him properly with due ceremonial. But in Calcutta he was a mere stranger and sojourner-in fact a fish out of water.

My friend, with his tall silk hat on, very gravely nodded. I need hardly say that according to English custom the hat ought to have been removed inside the room. But my friend did not dare to take it off for fear of detection; and Kailas Balm and his old servant Ganesh were sublimely unconscious of the breach of etiquette.

After a ten minutes' interview, which consisted chiefly of nodding the head, my friend rose to his feet to depart. The two flunkeys in livery, as had been planned beforehand, carried off in state the string of gold mohurs, the gold salver, the old ancestral shawl, the silver scent- sprinkler, and the otto-of-roses filigree box; they placed them ceremoniously in the carriage. Kailas Babu regarded this as the usual habit of Chota Lard Sahibs.

I was watching all the while from the next room. My sides were aching with suppressed laughter. When I could hold myself in no longer, I rushed into a further room, suddenly to discover, in a corner, a young girl sobbing as if her heart would break. When she saw my uproarious laughter she stood upright in passion, flashing the lightning of her big dark eyes in mine, and said with a tear-choked voice:

"Tell me! What harm has my grandfather done to you? Why have you come to deceive him? Why have you come here? Why"

She could say no more. She covered her face with her hands, and broke into sobs.

My laughter vanished in a moment. It had never occurred to me that there was anything but a supremely funny joke in this act of mine, and here I discovered that I had given the cruelest pain to this tenderest little heart. All the ugliness of my cruelty rose up to condemn me. I slunk out of the room in silence, like a kicked dog.

Hitherto I had only looked upon Kusum, the grand-daughter of Kailas Babu, as a somewhat worthless commodity in the marriage market, waiting in vain to attract a husband. But now I found, with a shock of surprise, that in the corner of that room a human heart was beating.

The whole night through I had very little sleep. My mind was in a tumult. On the next day, very early in the morning, I took all those stolen goods back to Kailas Babe's lodgings, wishing to hand them over in secret to the servant Ganesh. I waited outside the door, and, not finding any one, went upstairs to Kailas Babu's room. I heard from the passage Kusum asking her grandfather in the most winning voice: "Dada, dearest, do tell me all that the Chota Lord Sahib said to you yesterday. Don't leave out a single word. I am dying to hear it all over again."

And Dada needed no encouragement. His face beamed over with pride as he related all manner of praises, which the Lard Sahib had been good enough to utter concerning the ancient families of Nayanjore. The girl was seated before him, looking up into his face, and listening with rapt attention. She was determined, out of love for the old man, to play her part to the full.

My heart was deeply touched, and tears came to my eyes. I stood there in silence in the passage, while Thakur Dada finished all his embellishments of the Chota Lord Sahib's wonderful visit. When he left the room at last, I took the stolen goods and laid them at the feet of the girl and came away without a word.

Later in the day I called again to see Kailas Balm himself. According to our ugly modern custom, I had been in the habit of making no greeting at all to this old man when I came into the room. But on this day I made a low bow, and touched his feet. I am convinced the old man thought that the coming of the Chota Lord Sahib to his house was the cause of my new politeness. He was highly gratified by it, and an air of benign severity shone from his eyes. His friends had flocked in, and he had already begun to tell again at full length the story of the Lieutenant-Governor's visit with still further adornments of a most fantastic kind. The interview was already becoming an epic, both in quality and in length.

When the other visitors had taken their leave, I made my proposal to the old man in a humble manner. I told him that, " though I could never for a moment hope to be worthy of marriage connection with such an illustrious family, yet . . . etc. etc."

When I made clear my proposal of marriage, the old man embraced me, and broke out in a tumult of joy: "I am a poor man, and could never have expected such great good fortune."

That was the first and last time in his life that Kailas Babu confessed to being poor. It was also the first and last time in his life that he forgot, if only for a single moment, the ancestral dignity that belongs to the Babus of Nayanjore.

Kabuliwallah [The Fruitseller from Kabul]

My five years' old daughter Mini cannot live without chattering. I really believe that in all her life she has not wasted a minute in silence. Her mother is often vexed at this, and would stop her prattle, but I would not. To see Mini quiet is unnatural, and I cannot bear it long. And so my own talk with her is always lively.

One morning, for instance, when I was in the midst of the seventeenth chapter of my new novel, my little Mini stole into the room, and putting her hand into mine, said: "Father! Ramdayal the door-keeper calls a crow a krow! He doesn't know anything, does he?"

Before I could explain to her the differences of language in this world, she was embarked on the full tide of another subject. "What do you think, Father? Bhola says there is an elephant in the clouds, blowing water out of his trunk, and that is why it rains!"

And then, darting off anew, while I sat still making ready some reply to this last saying, "Father! what relation is Mother to you?"

"My dear little sister in the law!" I murmured involuntarily to myself, but with a grave face contrived to answer: "Go and play with Bhola, Mini! I am busy!"

The window of my room overlooks the road. The child had seated herself at my feet near my table, and was playing softly, drumming on her knees. I was hard at work on my seventeenth chapter, where Protrap Singh, the hero, had just caught Kanchanlata, the heroine, in his arms, and was about to escape with her by the third story window of the castle, when all of a sudden Mini left her play, and ran to the window, crying, "A Cabuliwallah! a Cabuliwallah!" Sure enough in the street below was a Cabuliwallah, passing slowly along. He wore the loose soiled clothing of his people, with a tall turban; there was a bag on his back, and he carried boxes of grapes in his hand.

I cannot tell what were my daughter's feelings at the sight of this man, but she began to call him loudly. "Ah!" I thought, "he will come in, and my seventeenth chapter will never be finished!" At which exact moment the Cabuliwallah turned, and looked up at the child. When she saw this, overcome by terror, she fled to her mother's protection, and disappeared. She had a blind belief that inside the bag, which the big man carried, there were perhaps two or three other children like herself. The pedlar meanwhile entered my doorway, and greeted me with a smiling face.

So precarious was the position of my hero and my heroine, that my first impulse was to stop and buy something, since the man had been called. I made some small purchases, and a conversation began about Abdurrahman, the Russians, she English, and the Frontier Policy.

As he was about to leave, he asked: "And where is the little girl, sir?"

And I, thinking that Mini must get rid of her false fear, had her brought out.

She stood by my chair, and looked at the Cabuliwallah and his bag. He offered her nuts and raisins, but she would not be tempted, and only clung the closer to me, with all her doubts increased.

This was their first meeting.

One morning, however, not many days later, as I was leaving the house, I was startled to find Mini, seated on a bench near the door, laughing and talking, with the great Cabuliwallah at her feet. In all her life, it appeared; my small daughter had never found so patient a listener, save her father. And already the corner of her little sari was stuffed with almonds and raisins, the gift of her visitor, "Why did you give her those?" I said, and taking out an eight-anna bit, I handed it to him. The man accepted the money without demur, and slipped it into his pocket.

Alas, on my return an hour later, I found the unfortunate coin had made twice its own worth of trouble! For the Cabuliwallah had given it to Mini, and her mother catching sight of the bright round object, had pounced on the child with: "Where did you get that eight-anna bit?"

"The Cabuliwallah gave it me," said Mini cheerfully.

"The Cabuliwallah gave it you!" cried her mother much shocked. "Oh, Mini! how could you take it from him?"

I, entering at the moment, saved her from impending disaster, and proceeded to make my own inquiries.

It was not the first or second time, I found, that the two had met. The Cabuliwallah had overcome the child's first terror by a judicious bribery of nuts and almonds, and the two were now great friends.

They had many quaint jokes, which afforded them much amusement. Seated in front of him, looking down on his gigantic frame in all her tiny dignity, Mini would ripple her face with laughter, and begin: "O Cabuliwallah, Cabuliwallah, what have you got in your bag?"

And he would reply, in the nasal accents of the mountaineer: "An elephant!" Not much cause for merriment, perhaps; but how they both enjoyed the witticism! And for me, this child's talk with a grown-up man had always in it something strangely fascinating.

Then the Cabuliwallah, not to be behindhand, would take his turn: "Well, little one, and when are you going to the father-in-law's house?"

Now most small Bengali maidens have heard long ago about the father-in-law's house; but we, being a little new-fangled, had kept these things from our child, and Mini at this question must have been a trifle bewildered. But she would not show it, and with ready tact replied: "Are you going there?"

Amongst men of the Cabuliwallah's class, however, it is well known that the words father-in-law's house have a double meaning. It is a euphemism for jail, the place where we are well cared for, at no expense to ourselves. In this sense would the sturdy pedlar take my daughter's question. "Ah," he would say, shaking his fist at an invisible policeman, "I will thrash my father-in-law!" Hearing this, and picturing the poor discomfited relative, Mini would go off into peals of laughter, in which her formidable friend would join.

These were autumn mornings, the very time of year when kings of old went forth to conquest; and I, never stirring from my little corner in Calcutta, would let my mind wander over the whole world. At the very name of another country, my heart would go out to it, and at the sight of a foreigner in the streets, I would fall to weaving a network of dreams, the mountains, the glens, and the forests of his distant home, with his cottage in its setting, and the free and independent life of far-away wilds. Perhaps the scenes of travel conjure themselves up before me, and pass and repass in my imagination all the more vividly, because I lead such a vegetable existence, that a call to travel would fall upon me like a thunderbolt. In the presence of this Cabuliwallah, I was immediately transported to the foot of arid mountain peaks, with narrow little defiles twisting in and out amongst their towering heights. I could see the string of camels bearing the merchandise, and the company of turbaned merchants, carrying some of their queer old firearms, and some of their spears, journeying downward towards the plains. I could see but at some such point Mini's mother would intervene, imploring me to "beware of that man."

Mini's mother is unfortunately a very timid lady. Whenever she hears a noise in the street, or sees people coming towards the house, she always jumps to the conclusion that they are either thieves, or drunkards, or snakes, or tigers, or malaria or cockroaches, or caterpillars, or an English sailor. Even after all these years of experience, she is not able to overcome her terror. So she was full of doubts about the Cabuliwallah, and used to beg me to keep a watchful eye on him.

I tried to laugh her fear gently away, but then she would turn round on me seriously, and ask me solemn questions.

Were children never kidnapped?

Was it, then, not true that there was slavery in Cabul?

Was it so very absurd that this big man should be able to carry off a tiny child?

I urged that, though not impossible, it was highly improbable. But this was not enough, and her dread persisted. As it was indefinite, however, it did not seem right to forbid the man the house, and the intimacy went on unchecked.

Once a year in the middle of January Rahmun, the Cabuliwallah, was in the habit of returning to his country, and as the time approached he would be very busy, going from house to house collecting his debts. This year, however, he could always find time to come and see Mini. It would have seemed to an outsider that there was some conspiracy between the two, for when he could not come in the morning, he would appear in the evening.

Even to me it was a little startling now and then, in the corner of a dark room, suddenly to surprise this tall, loose-garmented, much bebagged man; but when Mini would run in smiling, with her, "O! Cabuliwallah! Cabuliwallah!" and the two friends, so far apart in age, would subside into their old laughter and their old jokes, I felt reassured.

One morning, a few days before he had made up his mind to go, I was correcting my proof sheets in my study. It was chilly weather. Through the window the rays of the sun touched my feet, and the slight warmth was very welcome. It was almost eight o'clock, and the early pedestrians were returning home, with their heads covered. All at once, I heard an uproar in the street, and, looking out, saw Rahmun being led away bound between two policemen, and behind them a crowd of curious boys. There were blood-stains on the clothes of the Cabuliwallah, and one of the policemen carried a knife. Hurrying out, I stopped them, and enquired what it all meant. Partly from one, partly from another, I gathered that a certain neighbour had owed the pedlar something for a Rampuri shawl, but had falsely denied having bought it, and that in the course of the quarrel, Rahmun had struck him. Now in the heat of his excitement, the prisoner began calling his enemy all sorts of names, when suddenly in a verandah of my house appeared my little Mini, with her usual exclamation: "O Cabuliwallah! Cabuliwallah!" Rahmun's face lighted up as he turned to her. He had no bag under his arm today, so she could not discuss the elephant with him. She at once therefore proceeded to the next question: "Are you going to the father-in-law's house?" Rahmun laughed and said: "Just where I am going, little one!" Then seeing that the reply did not amuse the child, he held up his fettered hands. " Ali," he said, " I would have thrashed that old father-in-law, but my hands are bound!"

On a charge of murderous assault, Rahmun was sentenced to some years' imprisonment.

Time passed away, and he was not remembered. The accustomed work in the accustomed place was ours, and the thought of the once-free mountaineer spending his years in prison seldom or never occurred to us. Even my light-hearted Mini, I am ashamed to say, forgot her old friend. New companions filled her life. As she grew older, she spent more of her time with girls. So much time indeed did she spend with them that she came no more, as she used to do, to her father's room. I was scarcely on speaking terms with her.

Years had passed away. It was once more autumn and we had made arrangements for our Mini's marriage. It was to take place during the Puja Holidays. With Durga returning to Kailas, the light of our home also was to depart to her husband's house, and leave her father's in the shadow.

The morning was bright. After the rains, there was a sense of ablution in the air, and the sun-rays looked like pure gold. So bright were they that they gave a beautiful radiance even to the sordid brick walls of our Calcutta lanes. Since early dawn to-day the wedding-pipes had been sounding, and at each beat my own heart throbbed. The wail of the tune, Bhairavi, seemed to intensify my pain at the approaching separation. My Mini was to be married to-night.

From early morning noise and bustle had pervaded the house. In the courtyard the canopy had to be slung on its bamboo poles; the chandeliers with their tinkling sound must be hung in each room and verandah. There was no end of hurry and excitement. I was sitting in my study, looking through the accounts, when some one entered, saluting respectfully, and stood before me. It was Rahmun the Cabuliwallah. At first I did not recognise him. He had no bag, nor the long hair, nor the same vigour that he used to have. But he smiled, and I knew him again.

"When did you come, Rahmun?" I asked him.

"Last evening," he said, "I was released from jail."

The words struck harsh upon my ears. I had never before talked with one who had wounded his fellow, and my heart shrank within itself, when I realised this, for I felt that the day would have been better-omened had he not turned up.

"There are ceremonies going on," I said, "and I am busy. Could you perhaps come another day?"

At once he turned to go; but as he reached the door he hesitated, and said: "May I not see the little one, sir, for a moment?" It was his belief that Mini was still the same. He had pictured her running to him as she used, calling "O Cabuliwallah! Cabuliwallah!" He had imagined too that they would laugh and talk together, just as of old. In fact, in memory of former days he had brought, carefully wrapped up in paper, a few almonds and raisins and grapes, obtained somehow from a countryman, for his own little fund was dispersed.

I said again: "There is a ceremony in the house, and you will not be able to see any one to-day."

The man's face fell. He looked wistfully at me for a moment, said "Good morning," and went out. I felt a little sorry, and would have called him back, but I found he was returning of his own accord. He came close up to me holding out his offerings and said: "I brought these few things, sir, for the little one. Will you give them to her?"

I took them and was going to pay him, but he caught my hand and said: "You are very kind, sir! Keep me in your recollection. Do not offer me money! You have a little girl, I too have one like her in my own home. I think of her, and bring fruits to your child, not to make a profit for myself."

Saying this, he put his hand inside his big loose robe, and brought out a small and dirty piece of paper. With great care he unfolded this, and smoothed it out with both hands on my table. It bore the impression of a little band. Not a photograph. Not a drawing. The impression of an ink-smeared hand laid flat on the paper. This touch of his own little daughter had been always on his heart, as he had come year after year to Calcutta, to sell his wares in the streets.

Tears came to my eyes. I forgot that he was a poor Cabuli fruit-seller, while I was, but no, what was I more than he? He also was a father. That impression of the hand of his little Parbati in her distant mountain home reminded me of my own little Mini.

I sent for Mini immediately from the inner apartment. Many difficulties were raised, but I would not listen. Clad in the red silk of her wedding-day, with the sandal paste on her forehead, and adorned as a young bride, Mini came, and stood bashfully before me.

The Cabuliwallah looked a little staggered at the apparition. He could not revive their old friendship. At last he smiled and said: "Little one, are you going to your father-in-law's house?"

But Mini now understood the meaning of the word "father-in-law," and she could not reply to him as of old. She flushed up at the question, and stood before him with her bride-like face turned down.

I remembered the day when the Cabuliwallah and my Mini had first met, and I felt sad. When she had gone, Rahmun heaved a deep sigh, and sat down on the floor. The idea had suddenly come to him that his daughter too must have grown in this long time, and that he would have to make friends with her anew. Assuredly he would not find her, as he used to know her. And besides, what might not have happened to her in these eight years?

The marriage-pipes sounded, and the mild autumn sun streamed round us. But Rahmun sat in the little Calcutta lane, and saw before him the barren mountains of Afghanistan.

I took out a bank-note, and gave it to him, saying: "Go back to your own daughter, Rahmun, in your own country, and may the happiness of your meeting bring good fortune to my child!"

Having made this present, I had to curtail some of the festivities. I could not have the electric lights I had intended, nor the military band, and the ladies of the house were despondent at it. But to me the wedding feast was all the brighter for the thought that in a distant land a long-lost father met again with his only child.

The Victory

She was the Princess Ajita. And the court poet of King Narayan had never seen her. On the day he recited a new poem to the king he would raise his voice just to that pitch which could be heard by unseen hearers in the screened balcony high above the hall. He sent up his song towards the star-land out of his reach, where, circled with light, the planet who ruled his destiny shone unknown and out of ken.

He would espy some shadow moving behind the veil. A tinkling sound would come to his car from afar, and would set him dreaming of the ankles whose tiny golden bells sang at each step. Ah, the rosy red tender feet that walked the dust of the earth like God's mercy on the fallen! The poet had placed them on the altar of his heart, where he wove his songs to the tune of those golden bells. Doubt never arose in his mind as to whose shadow it was that moved behind the screen, and whose anklets they were that sang to the time of his beating heart.

Manjari, the maid of the princess, passed by the poet's house on her way to the river, and she never missed a day to have a few words with him on the sly. When she found the road deserted, and the shadow of dusk on the land, she would boldly enter his room, and sit at the corner of his carpet. There was a suspicion of an added care in the choice of the colour of her veil, in the setting of the flower in her hair.

People smiled and whispered at this, and they were not to blame. For Shekhar the poet never took the trouble to hide the fact that these meetings were a pure joy to him.

The meaning of her name was the spray of flowers. One must confess that for an ordinary mortal it was sufficient in its sweetness. But Shekhar made his own addition to this name, and called her the Spray of Spring Flowers. And ordinary mortals shook their heads and said, Ah, me!

In the spring songs that the poet sang the praise of the spray of spring flowers was conspicuously reiterated; and the king winked and smiled at him when he heard it, and the poet smiled in answer.

The king would put him the question; "Is it the business of the bee merely to hum in the court of the spring?"

The poet would answer; "No, but also to sip the honey of the spray of spring flowers."

And they all laughed in the king's hall. And it was rumoured that the Princess Akita also laughed at her maid's accepting the poet's name for her, and Manjari felt glad in her heart.

Thus truth and falsehood mingle in life, and to what God builds man adds his own decoration.

Only those were pure truths which were sung by the poet. The theme was Krishna, the lover god, and Radha, the beloved, the Eternal Man and the Eternal Woman, the sorrow that comes from the beginning of time, and the joy without end. The truth of these songs was tested in his inmost heart by everybody from the beggar to the king himself. The poet's songs were on the lips of all. At the merest glimmer of the moon and the faintest whisper of the summer breeze his songs would break forth in the land from windows and courtyards, from sailing-boats, from shadows of the wayside trees, in numberless voices.

Thus passed the days happily. The poet recited, the king listened, the hearers applauded, Manjari passed and repassed by the poet's room on her way to the river, the shadow flitted behind the screened balcony, and the tiny golden bells tinkled from afar.

Just then set forth from his home in the south a poet on his path of conquest. He came to King Narayan, in the kingdom of Amarapur. He stood before the throne, and uttered a verse in praise of the king. He had challenged all the court poets on his way, and his career of victory had been unbroken.

The king received him with honour, and said: "Poet, I offer you welcome."

Pundarik, the poet, proudly replied : "Sire, I ask for war."

Shekhar, the court poet of the king did not know how the battle of the muse was to be waged. He had no sleep at night. The mighty figure of the famous

Pundarik, his sharp nose curved like a scimitar, and his proud head tilted on one side, haunted the poet's vision in the dark.

With a trembling heart Shekhar entered the arena in the morning. The theatre was filled with the crowd.

The poet greeted his rival with a smile and a bow. Pundarik returned it with a slight toss of his head, and turned his face towards his circle of adoring followers with a meaning smile. Shekhar cast his glance towards the screened balcony high above, and saluted his lady in his mind, saying! "If I am the winner at the combat to-day, my lady, thy victorious name shall be glorified."

The trumpet sounded. The great crowd stood up, shouting victory to the king. The king, dressed in an ample robe of white, slowly came into the hall like a floating cloud of autumn, and sat on his throne.

Pundarik stood up, and the vast hall became still. With his head raised high and chest expanded, he began in his thundering voice to recite the praise of King Narayan. His words burst upon the walls of the hall like breakers of the sea, and seemed to rattle against the ribs of the listening crowd. The skill with which he gave varied meanings to the name Narayan, and wove each letter of it through the web of his verses in all mariner of combinations, took away the breath of his amazed hearers.

For some minutes after he took his seat his voice continued to vibrate among the numberless pillars of the king's court and in thousands of speechless hearts. The learned professors who had come from distant lands raised their right hands, and cried, Bravo !

The king threw a glance on Shekhar's face, and Shekhar in answer raised for a moment his eyes full of pain towards his master, and then stood up like a stricken deer at bay. His face was pale, his bashfulness was almost that of a woman, his slight youthful figure, delicate in its outline, seemed like a tensely strung vina ready to break out in music at the least touch.

His head was bent, his voice was low, when he began. The first few verses were almost inaudible. Then he slowly raised his head, and his clear sweet voice rose into the sky like a quivering flame of fire. He began with the ancient legend of the kingly line lost in the haze of the past, and brought it down through its long course of heroism and matchless generosity to the present age. He fixed his gaze on the king's face, and all the vast and unexpressed love of the people for the royal house rose like incense in his song, and enwreathed the throne on all sides. These were his last words when, trembling, he took his seat: "My master, I may be beaten in play of words, but not in my love for thee,"

Tears filled the eyes of the hearers, and the stone walls shook with cries of victory.

Mocking this popular outburst of feeling, with an august shake of his head and a contemptuous sneer, Pundarik stood up, and flung this question to the assembly; "What is there superior to words?" In a moment the hall lapsed into silence again.

Then with a marvellous display of learning, he proved that the Word was in the beginning, that the Word was God. He piled up quotations from scriptures, and built a high altar for the Word to be seated above all that there is in heaven and in earth. He repeated that question in his mighty voice: "What is there superior to words?"

Proudly he looked around him. None dared to accept his challenge, and he slowly took his seat like a lion who had just made a full meal of its victim. The pandits shouted, Bravo ! The king remained silent with wonder, and the poet Shekhar felt himself of no account by the side of this stupendous learning. The assembly broke up for that day.

Next day Shekhar began his song. It was of that day when the pipings of love's flute startled for the first time the hushed air of the Vrinda forest. The shepherd women did not know who was the player or whence came the music. Sometimes it seemed to come from the heart of the south wind, and sometimes from the straying clouds of the hilltops. It came with a message of tryst from the land of the sunrise, and it floated from the verge of sunset with its sigh of sorrow. The stars seemed to be the stops of the instrument that flooded the dreams of the night with melody. The music seemed to burst all at once from all sides, from fields and groves, from the shady lanes and lonely roads, from the melting blue of the sky, from the shimmering green of the grass. They neither knew its meaning nor could they find words to give utterance to the desire of their hearts. Tears filled their eyes, and their life seemed to long for a death that would be its consummation.

Shekhar forgot his audience, forgot the trial of his strength with a rival. He stood alone amid his thoughts that rustled and quivered round him like leaves in a summer breeze, and sang the Song of the Flute. He had in his mind the vision of an image that had taken its shape from a shadow, and the echo of a faint tinkling sound of a distant footstep.

He took his seat. His hearers trembled with the sadness of an indefinable delight, immense and vague, and they forgot to applaud him. As this feeling died away Pundarik stood up before the throne and challenged his rival to define who was this Lover and who was the Beloved. He arrogantly looked around him, he smiled at his followers and then put the question again : "Who is Krishna, the lover, and who is Radha, the beloved?"

Then he began to analyse the roots of those names, and various interpretations of their meanings. He brought before the bewildered audience all the intricacies of the different schools of metaphysics with consummate skill. Each letter of those names he divided from its fellow, and then pursued them with a relentless logic till they fell to the dust in confusion, to be caught up again and restored to a meaning never before imagined by the subtlest of word-mongers.

The pandits were in ecstasy; they applauded vociferously ; and the crowd followed them, deluded into the certainty that they had witnessed, that day, the last shred of the curtains of Truth torn to pieces before their eyes by a prodigy of intellect. The performance of his tremendous feat so delighted them that they forgot to ask themselves if there was any truth behind it after all.

The king's mind was overwhelmed with wonder. The atmosphere was completely cleared of all illusion of music, and the vision of the world around seemed to be changed from its freshness of tender green to the solidity of a high road levelled and made hard with crushed stones.

To the people assembled their own poet appeared a mere boy in comparison with this giant, who walked with such case, knocking down difficulties at each step in the world of words and thoughts. It became evident to them for the first time that the poems Shekhar wrote were absurdly simple, and it must be a mere accident that they did not write them themselves. They were neither new, nor difficult, nor instructive, nor necessary.

The king tried to goad his poet with keen glances, silently inciting him to make a final effort. But Shekhar took no notice, and remained fixed to his seat.

The king in anger came down from his throne, took off his pearl chain and put it on Pundarik's head. Everybody in the hall cheered. From the upper balcony came a slight sound of the movements of rustling robes and waist-chains hung with golden bells. Shekhar rose from his seat and left the hall.

It was a dark night of waning moon. The poet Shekhar took down his MSS. from his shelves and heaped them on the floor. Some of them contained his earliest writings, which he had almost forgotten. He turned over the pages, reading passages here and there. They all seemed to him poor and trivial, mere words and childish rhymes!

One by one he tore his books to fragments, and threw them into a vessel containing fire, and said: "To thee, to thee, O my beauty, my fire! Thou hast been burning in my heart all these futile years. If my life were a piece of gold it would come out of its trial brighter, but it is a trodden turf of grass, and nothing remains of it but this handful of ashes."

The night wore on. Shekhar opened wide his windows. He spread upon his bed the white flowers that he loved, the jasmines, tuberoses and chrysanthemums, and brought into his bedroom all the lamps he had in his house and lighted them. Then mixing with honey the juice of some poisonous root he drank it and lay down on his bed.

Golden anklets tinkled in the passage outside the door, and a subtle perfume came into the room with the breeze.

The poet, with his eyes shut, said; "My lady, have you taken pity upon your servant at last and come to see him?"

The answer came in a sweet voice "My poet, I have come."

Shekhar opened his eyes, and saw before his bed the figure of a woman.

His sight was dim and blurred. And it seemed to him that the image made of a shadow that he had ever kept throned in the secret shrine of his heart had come into the outer world in his last moment to gaze upon his face.

The woman said; "I am the Princess Ajita."

The poet with a great effort sat up on his bed.

The princess whispered into his ear: "The king has not done you justice. It was you who won at the combat, my poet, and I have come to crown you with the crown of victory."

She took the garland of flowers from her own neck, and put it on his hair, and the poet fell down upon his bed stricken by death.

Rabindranath Tagore: A Biography

Rabindranath Tagore (1861-1941) is an Indian poet, playwright, novelist, composer, painter and a national icon of his country. His profuse literary production ranges from collections of poems such as *Manasi* (1890), *Gitanjali* (1910) and Patraput (1936) to drama such as *Visarjan* (1890), *Raja* (1910), *Muktadhara* (1922) and *Chandalika* (1938) and even numerous musical compositions and songs. In addition, Tagore's publications include a number of novels and several volumes of short stories including his widely appreciated *Gora* (1910) along with *Chaturanga* (1916) and *Ghare-Baire* (1916). The latter is one of his works that were adapted to cinema.

Born in Calcutta, India, to a well-off family, Rabindranath Tagore was raised and educated mainly by servants. His father Devendranath Tagore is a saint and a religious leader of the Adi Dham faith and the Brahmo sect founded by the family's patriarchs. Young Rabindranath Tagore's home was animated by discussions of literary publications, arts, theatrical performances and classical music where most of his 14 siblings were much interested in arts, poetry, music, philosophy and theatre, such as his older sister, Swarnakumari Devi, the renowned Indian novelist, poet and musician.

In addition to such a supportive environment for artistic appreciation and creativity, Tagore's father made him discover language, literature, history and poetry, taking him for long journeys around the country. In 1873, they both left home for the hill station at Dalhousie. Named after the British Governor-General Lord Dalhousie who used to visit it during his summer holidays, the station is surrounded by captivating green hills and heaven-like vistas. During the months spent there, Tagore must have found in the station's assortments of Hindu art and temples, along with the European architecture of its summer residences, a magnificent blending of East and West.

Readers of Tagore's poetry, novels and short stories, such as "The Fruitseller from Kabul," to name but a sample, can surely detect in their imagery and emotional outlets the influence of Dalhousie's breath-taking sceneries and verdure. Tagore's journey with his father was mainly meant to be a necessary stage towards intellectual and moral maturity and individuation. The lessons that the father transmitted to the son in such an inspirational spot were not only meant to be informational lessons but also spiritual ones. Indeed, being a very respected spiritual figure who wished to hand on the torch to younger disciples,

Tagore's father inculcated in him mystical yearnings for spiritual knowledge and existential meaning.

It is, however, noteworthy that despite his conspicuous lust for knowledge, Tagore hated the "yoke" of formal education and thought that classroom teaching could only muffle young people's innate and instinctive thirst for discovery and adventure. The two long journeys that he had with his father only reinforced this attitude as they helped nourish his love for nature and the divine. Helped by his father, his brother Hemendranath and the house servants, Tagore studied language, literature, mathematics, geography and history and practiced different sports at home and in the family's manor. When his father sent him to London to study law in 1878, he quickly left University College London and chose to study language, literature and music by himself. Two years later, he travelled back to India without getting the formal degree he was sent for.

Tagore expressed in many an occasion his belief that teaching should arouse curiosity rather than be informative and he strove to put his ideas into practice particularly by founding the Visva-Bharati school, which has now become the Visva-Bharati University, where he established the "brahmacharya" educational system. The main characteristic of Tagore's educational conception was to have teachers incite their students to discover and learn through employing intellectual and spiritual motivational strategies.

As for his writings, Tagore was a genuine prodigy who started weaving his earliest verses by the age of eight in the family's Calcutta residence. A few years later, he pseudonymously published his first collection of poems which was an astounding success to the point that local critics thought the compilation to belong to the 17th-century poet Bhānusimha. He soon shifted to writing short stories and plays to achieve considerable fame in the region. While all his writings were in his native Bengali language, he eventually decided to address Western readers by translating some of his own works into English.

The English versions of his poetic works such as *Manasi* (1890), *Gitimalya* (1914) and mainly what is today considered in the West as his magnum opus, *Gitanjali* (1910), quickly gained ground among Western literary circles. Such works were read, reviewed and prefaced by leading literary figures of the time like William Butler Yeats and Ezra Pound. Tagore soon became an oriental icon who stands for India's literary, spiritual and cultural heritage. In 1913, the relatively small part of his works discovered by the West earned him the Nobel Prize in Literature. In 1915, he was also knighted by the British Crown for his literary achievements.

Once famous in the West, Tagore toured Britain and the United States and lectured in many other European and non-European countries to meet and interact with important celebrities around the world including the celebrated German-born physicist Albert Einstein, Thomas Mann, George Bernard Shaw and H.G. Wells, among many others.

Politically, while Tagore's commitment manifested in his harsh criticism of nationalist extremism and in his avant-garde and reformatory positions at home, he denounced imperialism and advocated universalism and internationalism in the world. In India, he was known for his rejection of the culture of victimhood and for inciting his countrymen to have the courage of assuming the responsibilities of their misfortunes. He saw that salvation could only be realized through education and self-help. In addition to that, Tagore was also socially active in his homeland, supporting students and the poor. As for foreign affairs, Tagore denounced British colonialism and even renounced the honor previously granted by the British Crown in protest against the 1919 Jallianwala Bagh massacre.

Such political views were explicitly expressed in some of Tagore's writings and musical compositions, two of which were chosen by India and Bangladesh as national anthems. His friend Mahatma Gandhi, the celebrated leader of the Indian nationalist movement, expressed his appreciation of these compositions and was said to favor the "Ekla Chalo Re" hymn.

Towards the twilight of his career, Tagore developed new interests, mainly in arts, paintings and sciences. This is mainly expressed in stories like *Se* (1937) and *Tin Sangi* (1940) as well as in his collection of essays entitled *Visva-Parichay* (1937) which represents a literary man's exploration of the fields of astronomy, physics and biology. He even took up drawing and painting at a late age and organized exhibitions of his works in Paris and other cities.
Towards the end of the 1930s, old Rabindranath Tagore's health started to deteriorate until he died on August 7th, 1941, leaving a gigantic oeuvre of numerous volumes of fine poetry, hundreds of texts, short stories, novels, plays, paintings, doodles, more than two thousand songs, two autobiographies and numerous travelogues, essays and lectures.

Tagore's life experience had taught him that divisions between human beings are nothing but an unpleasant mirage. Generally, his oeuvre invites and incites its readers to the exploration of the Other, the exploration of the Self. The following extract from his masterpiece *Gitanjali* may serve as a perfect illustration of Tagore's philosophical vision:

The time that my journey takes is long and the way of it long.

I came out on the chariot of the first gleam of light, and pursued my voyage through the wildernesses of worlds leaving my track on many a star and planet. It is the most distant course that comes nearest to thyself, and that training is the most intricate which leads to the utter simplicity of a tune.

The traveller has to knock at every alien door to come to his own, and one has to wander through all the outer worlds to reach the innermost shrine at the end. My eyes strayed far and wide before I shut them and said 'Here art thou!'

The question and the cry 'Oh, where?' melt into tears of a thousand streams and deluge the world with the flood of the assurance 'I am!' (Song XII)

Rabindranath Tagore

Rabindranath Tagore (1861-1941) is an Indian poet, playwright, novelist, composer, painter and a national icon of his country. His profuse literary production ranges from collections of poems such as *Manasi* (1890), *Gitanjali* (1910) and Patraput (1936) to drama such as *Visarjan* (1890), *Raja* (1910), *Muktadhara* (1922) and *Chandalika* (1938) and even numerous musical compositions and songs. In addition, Tagore's publications include a number of novels and several volumes of short stories including his widely appreciated *Gora* (1910) along with *Chaturanga* (1916) and *Ghare-Baire* (1916). The latter is one of his many works that were adapted to cinema.

Born in Calcutta, India, to a well-off family, Rabindranath Tagore was raised and educated mainly by servants. His father Devendranath Tagore is a saint and a religious leader of the Adi Dham faith and the Brahmo sect founded by the family's patriarchs. Young Rabindranath Tagore's home was animated by discussions of literary publications, arts, theatrical performances and classical music where most of his 14 siblings were much interested in arts, poetry, music, philosophy and theatre, such as his older sister, Swarnakumari Devi, the renowned Indian novelist, poet and musician.

In addition to such a supportive environment for artistic appreciation and creativity, Tagore's father made him discover language, literature, history and poetry, taking him for long journeys around the country. In 1873, they both left home for the hill station at Dalhousie. Named after the British Governor-General Lord Dalhousie who used to visit it during his summer holidays, the station is surrounded by captivating green hills and heaven-like vistas. During the months spent there, Tagore must have found in the station's assortments of Hindu art and temples, along with the European architecture of its summer residences, a magnificent blending of East and West.

Readers of Tagore's poetry, novels and short stories, such as "The Fruitseller from Kabul," to name but a sample, can surely detect in their imagery and emotional outlets the influence of Dalhousie's breath-taking sceneries and verdure. Tagore's journey with his father was mainly meant to be a necessary stage towards intellectual and moral maturity and individuation. The lessons that the father transmitted to the son in such an inspirational spot were not only meant to be informational lessons but also spiritual ones. Indeed, being a very respected spiritual figure who wished to hand on the torch to younger disciples, Tagore's father inculcated in him mystical yearnings for spiritual knowledge and existential meaning.

It is, however, noteworthy that despite his conspicuous lust for knowledge, Tagore hated the "yoke" of formal education and thought that classroom teaching could only muffle young people's innate and instinctive thirst for discovery and adventure. The two long journeys that he had with his father only reinforced this attitude as they helped nourish his love for nature and the divine. Helped by his father, his brother Hemendranath and the house servants, Tagore studied language, literature, mathematics, geography and history and practiced different sports at home and in the family's manor. When his father sent him to London to study law in 1878, he quickly left University College London and chose to study language, literature and music by himself. Two years later, he travelled back to India without getting the formal degree he was sent for.

Tagore expressed in many an occasion his belief that teaching should arouse curiosity rather than be informative and he strove to put his ideas into practice particularly by founding the Visva-Bharati school, which has now become the Visva-Bharati University, where he established the "brahmacharya" educational system. The main characteristic of Tagore's educational conception was to have teachers incite their students to discover and learn through employing intellectual and spiritual motivational strategies.

As for his writings, Tagore was a genuine prodigy who started weaving his earliest verses by the age of eight in the family's Calcutta residence. A few years later, he pseudonymously published his first collection of poems which was an astounding success to the point that local critics thought the compilation to belong to the 17th-century poet Bhanusimha. He soon shifted to writing short stories and plays to achieve considerable fame in the region. While all his writings were in his native Bengali language, he eventually decided to address Western readers by translating some of his own works into English.

The English versions of his poetic works such as *Manasi* (1890), *Gitimalya* (1914) and mainly what is today considered in the West as his magnum opus, *Gitanjali* (1910), quickly gained ground among Western literary circles. Such works were read, reviewed and prefaced by leading literary figures of the time like William Butler Yeats and Ezra Pound. Tagore soon became an oriental icon who stands for India's literary, spiritual and cultural heritage. In 1913, the relatively small part of his works discovered by the West earned him the Nobel Prize in Literature. In 1915, he was also knighted by the British Crown for his literary achievements.

Once famous in the West, Tagore toured Britain and the United States and lectured in many other European and non-European countries to meet and interact with important celebrities around the world including the celebrated German-born physicist Albert Einstein, Thomas Mann, George Bernard Shaw and H.G. Wells, among many others.

Politically, while Tagore's commitment manifested in his harsh criticism of nationalist extremism and in his avant-garde and reformatory positions at home, he denounced imperialism and advocated universalism and internationalism in the world. In India, he was known for his rejection of the culture of victimhood and for inciting his countrymen to have the courage of assuming the responsibilities of their misfortunes. He saw that salvation could only be realized through education and self-help. In addition to that, Tagore was also socially active in his homeland, supporting students and the poor. As for foreign affairs, Tagore denounced British colonialism and even renounced the honor previously granted by the British Crown in protest against the 1919 Jallianwala Bagh massacre.

Such political views were explicitly expressed in some of Tagore's writings and musical compositions, two of which were chosen by India and Bangladesh as national anthems. His friend Mahatma Gandhi, the celebrated leader of the Indian nationalist movement, expressed his appreciation of these compositions and was said to favor the "Ekla Chalo Re" hymn.

Towards the twilight of his career, Tagore developed new interests, mainly in arts, paintings and sciences. This is mainly expressed in stories like *Se* (1937) and *Tin Sangi* (1940) as well as in his collection of essays entitled *Visva-Parichay* (1937) which represents a literary man's exploration of the fields of astronomy, physics and biology. He even took up drawing and painting at a late age and organized exhibitions of his works in Paris and other cities.

Towards the end of the 1930s, old Rabindranath Tagore's health started to deteriorate until he died on August 7th, 1941, leaving a gigantic oeuvre of numerous volumes of fine poetry, hundreds of texts, short stories, novels, plays, paintings, doodles, more than two thousand songs, two autobiographies and numerous travelogues, essays and lectures.

Tagore's life experience had taught him that divisions between human beings are nothing but an unpleasant mirage. Generally, his oeuvre invites and incites its readers to the exploration of the Other, the exploration of the Self. The following extract from his masterpiece *Gitanjali* may serve as a perfect illustration of Tagore's philosophical vision:

The time that my journey takes is long and the way of it long.
I came out on the chariot of the first gleam of light, and pursued my voyage
through the wildernesses of worlds leaving my track on many a star and planet.
It is the most distant course that comes nearest to thyself, and that training is the
most intricate which leads to the utter simplicity of a tune.
The traveller has to knock at every alien door to come to his own, and one has
to wander through all the outer worlds to reach the innermost shrine at the end.
My eyes strayed far and wide before I shut them and said 'Here art thou!'
The question and the cry 'Oh, where?' melt into tears of a thousand streams and
deluge the world with the flood of the assurance 'I am!' (Song XII)

www.ingramcontent.com/pod-product-compliance
Lightning Source LLC
Chambersburg PA
CBHW061458170626
46811CB00004B/1571

* 9 7 8 1 7 8 0 0 0 6 8 8 8 *